D1587508

EVERYMAN'S LIBRARY

EVERYMAN,
I WILL GO WITH THEE,
AND BE THY GUIDE,
IN THY MOST NEED
TO GO BY THY SIDE

JOSEPH ROTH

REBELLION

TRANSLATED FROM THE GERMAN
BY MICHAEL HOFMANN

WITH AN INTRODUCTION
BY CAROLIN DUTTLINGER

EVERYMAN'S LIBRARY
Alfred A. Knopf New York London Toronto

407

THIS IS A BORZOI BOOK
PUBLISHED BY ALFRED A. KNOPF

First included in Everyman's Library, 2022
First published as *Die Rebellion* in 1924 by Die Schmiede, Berlin
Copyright © 1956, 1975, 1989, and 1997 by Verlag Kiepenheuer &
Witsch, Cologne, and Verlag Allert de Lange, Amsterdam
English translation copyright © 1999 by Michael Hofmann
Published by arrangement with St. Martin's Publishing Group,
New York, and Granta Books, London

Introduction copyright © 2022 by Carolin Duttlinger
Bibliography and Chronology copyright © 2022 by Everyman's Library

All rights reserved. Published in the United States by Alfred A. Knopf,
a division of Penguin Random House LLC, New York, and in Canada by
Penguin Random House Canada Limited, Toronto. Distributed by
Penguin Random House LLC, New York. Published in the United
Kingdom by Everyman's Library, 50 Albemarle Street, London
W1S 4BD and distributed by Penguin Random House UK,
20 Vauxhall Bridge Road, London SW1V 2SA.

everymanslibrary.com
www.everymanslibrary.co.uk

ISBN: 978-0-593-53412-0 (US)
978-1-84159-407-1 (UK)

A CIP catalogue reference for this book is available from the
British Library

Typography by Peter B. Willberg
Book design by Barbara de Wilde and Carol Devine Carson
Typeset in the UK by Input Data Services Ltd, Isle Abbotts, Somerset
Printed and bound in Germany by GGP Media GmbH, Pössneck

REBELLION

INTRODUCTION

———

Born in 1894, Joseph Roth grew up in the shtetl of Brody in East Galicia (modern-day Ukraine), on the outer reaches of the Habsburg Empire. From 1913, he studied German literature and philosophy, first in nearby Lemberg (Lviv) and then in Vienna. A pacifist, he initially opposed the war but subsequently felt ashamed of his own stance, and so in 1916 he volunteered to join the Austrian army and served on the Eastern Front as a war correspondent. This experience shaped his later career. After World War I, Roth returned to Vienna and started writing for various newspapers. Two years later, he moved to Berlin where he quickly established himself as one of the leading journalists of his time. His principal association was with the centre-left *Frankfurter Zeitung*, for which he travelled across Europe as its arts correspondent.

Die Rebellion was Roth's third novel, following the unfinished *Das Spinnennetz* (*The Spider's Web*, 1923) and *Hotel Savoy* (1924). All three novels were first serialized in newspapers, and all three of them feature protagonists who have returned from the war. *Rebellion* starts at the tail end of the war; it tells the story of Andreas Pum, who has been discharged from the army with an amputated leg and an iron cross. At the beginning, we meet him as he and fellow invalids are being treated at the '24th Military Hospital'. Though the town is only a half-hour's walk away, it is out of reach for the injured men, who are blind or unable to walk. They are in limbo, waiting to be discharged back into society and into an uncertain future.

Andreas, though, is relatively content.

He had lost a leg and been given a medal. There were many who had no medal, even though they had lost more than merely a leg. They had lost both arms or both legs. Or they would be bedridden for the rest of their lives, because there was something the matter with their spinal fluid. Andreas Pum rejoiced when he saw the sufferings of the others.

vii

For Andreas, the suffering of others is a validation of his own moral superiority, confirmed by a just society and indeed of a just God, who metes out

shrapnel, amputations, and medals to the deserving. Viewed in the correct light, the loss of a leg wasn't so very bad, and the joy of receiving a medal was considerable. An invalid might enjoy the respect of the world. An invalid with a medal could depend on that of the government.

The government is something that overlies man like the sky overlies the earth. What comes from it may be good or ill, but it cannot be other than great and all-powerful, unknowable and mysterious, even though on occasion it may be understood by an ordinary person.

In these troubled times, such a holistic world view, in which the divine and the worldly order do not oppose but rather stabilize and mirror each other, may seem surprising. On closer inspection, though, his is a defensive stance, fed by fear and even hatred of those who challenge the status quo. In Andreas's mind, anyone who rages against the war or the government is a 'heathen'. This morally loaded term is applied not only to revolutionaries, thieves and drunks, but also to the weakest in society, namely those suffering from (physical or mental) illness:

How many such specimens Andreas could have produced from his hospital time alone, where the wards were acrawl with godless individuals! How many had ugly, disfiguring, and highly infectious diseases! ... Whereas Andreas was pure in body and spirit, he had gone through life as though inoculated against sins and sufferings, an obedient son to his father, and later on a briskly compliant subordinate to his superiors.

While those who are ill, weak or angry have only themselves to blame, Andreas casts himself in a glowing light, as a beacon of morality, 'devout, mild, law-abiding, and dwelling in complete harmony with divine and human laws'. Here, as in the previous passages, the narrative blurs the line between worldly and divine authority. This, incidentally, is the only point where the text mentions Andreas's father, but this figure remains strangely abstract, one piece in the bigger jigsaw of social authority.

Andreas's attitude is chilling but not unusual for the time. It reflects one of the keywords of the Weimar period, namely the notion of *Daseinskampf*, of life as the perpetual struggle of all against all. In this social Darwinist world view, another person's misfortune is equivalent to one's own ascent. This position marks the starting-point of a narrative in which Andreas's belief and indeed his entire identity gradually unravel. However, while he ends an aged and broken man, his downfall and humiliation will bring about his spiritual rebirth and with it a more compassionate outlook.

Roth's fast-paced novel falls roughly into two parts. The first six chapters trace Andreas's ascent from an invalid to a happily married man respected by society. In the seventh chapter, the narrative suddenly shifts from his story to that of Herr Arnold, a philandering businessman, who will cause Andreas's downfall. That said, long before this turning-point we get indications of worse to come. The narrative is filled with a sense of foreboding, with subtle signs that Andreas's optimism and faith in God and the system are blinkered and in fact dangerous.

One site where this sense of foreboding manifests itself is the body. The new methods of industrial warfare had inflicted unprecedented damage on soldiers' bodies, and the fate of the damaged survivors became the subject of heated political debate between pacifists and advocates of the military and the monarchy. Left-wing commentators in particular drew attention to soldiers' horrific injuries to make the case against warfare. One famous example of this debate is Ernst Friedrich's bestselling photobook *Krieg dem Kriege* (*War against War*, 1924), published in the same year as Roth's novel, which assembles graphic photographs of mutilated bodies. These same bodies also feature in Expressionist art – in the paintings of Otto Dix, George Grosz and Ernst Ludwig Kirchner, while Expressionist drama staged the trauma of the war through surreal and nightmarish scenes. The protagonist of Ernst Toller's 1923 play *Der deutsche Hinkemann* (*The German Hinkemann*) has lost not his limbs but his genitals in the war, while former soldier Karl Thomas in Toller's 1927 play *Hoppla, wir leben!* (*Oops, We're Alive!*) starts off in a mental asylum and ends up committing suicide. Compared to these characters, Roth's Andreas Pum seems strangely untroubled by his injury.

True, he has lost a leg, but he is the fastest and fittest among the patients, and has even been awarded an iron cross in recognition of his bravery. Later in the novel Andreas recalls his traumatic injury with curious understatement. Playing on the euphemism of having 'lost' his limb, he describes how he let his lower leg 'drop' out of the knee joint ('[es] aus dem Kniegelenk fallen ließ'). But the narrative belies his apparent stoicism as it keeps returning to his stump and missing limb, which become a barometer of Andreas's changing fortunes. The prosthesis promised to him by the head doctor never arrives. Instead, Andreas has to make do with a wooden peg which is strapped to the stump. In his early days as a hurdy-gurdy man, he is troubled by phantom pain, particularly before a rainy day, but after his wedding, the pain miraculously disappears, as 'in its freshly padded extension, his stump was as warmly cushioned as if it were in the hollow of a woman's loving hand'. Revealingly, his pain reappears in the night after his clash with Herr Arnold and the authorities, and causes his wife to leave him for another man.

His missing leg hurt him again, for the first time in a long time. He unbuckled his leg, and felt his stump. It had the shape of a flattened cone. The flesh was crisscrossed with faint cracks and hollows. When Andreas put his hand on it, the pain eased. But the other pain in his heart was unappeasable.

Here, as in Sigmund Freud's case studies of hysterical and neurotic patients, the body betrays what is repressed by the (conscious) mind. Indeed, it is only in prison that Andreas Pum can admit to himself that in losing a leg, he 'lost a piece of himself and carried on living'.

The close but oblique connection between body and mind becomes more readily apparent in the second chapter when Andreas faces the medical commission who are to decide his fate. Being a *Zitterer* or 'trembler', that is, a soldier suffering from shell shock, is a much-coveted condition among the patients, for it allows the sufferer to remain in the hospital, sheltered from destitution. Only one of the inmates, the blacksmith Bossi, is suffering from this condition; he is watched with a mixture of awe and envy by the other patients, including Pum, who tries to emulate his trembling. But when he is examined, this tremor becomes real:

Suddenly, Andreas began to shake. He saw the head of the commission, a senior officer with a gold collar and a blond beard. Beard, face and uniform collar blended into an impression of white and gold. 'Another shell-shock case,' somebody said. The crutches in Andreas's hands began to skitter across the floor all by themselves. A couple of orderlies leaped to their feet to assist him.

Andreas's trembling is no sham, no performance, but a spontaneous response. As a result, he is granted the coveted barrel-organ permit, but the experience leaves him faintly troubled, as he later toys with the idea of seeing a doctor. Indeed, this episode is a warning sign, a foretaste of things to come, for it foreshadows that fateful encounter on the tram when Andreas once again loses control over his mind and body when faced with figures of authority.

First, though, Andreas feels happy and reassured, ready to take on the world. He calls his trembling fit a 'miracle', and this word is used once again at the start of chapter six, after he has fallen in love with the newly widowed Katharina Blumich. Their courtship is very quick; Andreas moves in with her only a few weeks after the death of her husband. Their marriage gives Andreas a sense of home and sexual fulfilment. Most importantly, it gives him a family. As the narrator reveals, it is not Katharina who is dearest to him: 'He loves everything in the world, and most of all two – are they things or people? They belong together, though they're of different species. Andreas loves Anni and he loves Mooli, he loves the little girl and the donkey.' While the donkey Mooli pulls the cart with his barrel organ on it, Andreas is particularly fond of Katharina's daughter, five-year-old Anni, whose warm little hand he can feel in his on his 'long and lonely walk home'. Here, the text shows us a different side to Andreas: not the hostile and suspicious former soldier, but a family man who experiences the 'beneficent, healing warmth' of love blossom inside himself.

That said, his new role as an organ-grinder continues to feed Andreas's sense of self-importance and superiority. Here, however, the narrative also reveals the brittleness of this stance. The hurdy-gurdy permit which he has been granted by the authorities takes on an almost obsessive importance for him:

Andreas Pum keeps his permit in his wallet, which used to be the leather cover of a notebook that he salvaged from a rubbish heap that he walks past every day. With his permit in his pocket, a man may walk serenely through the streets of the world, though they be swarming with policemen. One need fear no danger; indeed, there is none to fear. No denunciation from any ill-disposed neighbor need concern us. We write the authorities a postcard and tell them what it's about. We keep our remarks brief and to the point. Our permit puts us on a similar footing to the authorities. The government allows us to play wherever and whenever we please. We may set up our barrel organs on busy corners. Of course, within five minutes the police are there. Let them come! Surrounded by a ring of anxious onlookers, we pull out our permit.

This passage illustrates Roth's virtuosic narrative technique of revealing the doubt and anxiety which lurk underneath the surface of Andreas Pum's apparent confidence. The long list of benefits granted by the permit and the repeated reference to the many possible dangers which are fended off by it have the opposite effect to what is intended by this inner monologue. It reveals Pum's deep-rooted sense of uncertainty in a world populated not only by 'ill-disposed' neighbours but also by even more dangerous figures of authority – the police officers who are 'swarming' across the city. His licence is the bedrock of Pum's identity, a shield in a dangerous world, but the emphatic statement that 'One need fear no danger; indeed, there is none to fear' rings hollow, as it reveals his barely suppressed panic in the face of a dangerous reality. The fact that he keeps the licence in a repurposed wallet salvaged from the rubbish heap or *Misthaufen* underlines the flimsiness of this document and the status it conveys. More fundamentally, the passage illustrates the precariousness of Pum's world view, where good (God, the state) prevails over evil. As this passage shows, even the supposedly 'good' authorities are subliminally seen as a threat from early on in the narrative. Indeed, in the novel the entire city is cast as a danger zone, even a potential death trap. The narrator tells us that 'the street is our enemy', where, in winter, 'we fall, robbed of our mobility by the cold'. This sentiment is in tune with the febrile mood of the times, which many contemporaries experienced as a perpetual state of emergency.

Another interesting aspect of the novel illustrated here is its fluid use of narrative voice, and specifically the recurring shifts from the third person into the more inclusive 'we'. The precise identity of this collective voice is never disclosed and remains fluid all the way through the novel: in general terms, this narrative 'we' invites the reader to identify with the protagonist, though it also draws us into his paranoid mindset and futile efforts at self-reassurance.

If his permit is one of Andreas's most prized possessions then the barrel organ is the other. The instrument plays eight different tunes, which include folk songs and a waltz as well as the national anthem. By turning the handle faster or slower, he is able to give his limited repertoire either military pizzazz or the more languorous air of a funeral march. Indeed, although it is only mechanical, he 'came to love his instrument and held a dialogue with it that only he could understand. Andreas Pum was a true musician'. Even more attractive than its tunes, however, is the picture which is painted onto the side, showing children who are turned into does by an 'evil woman'. Andreas is fascinated by this fairy-tale image and its bright colours, and later pores over it with Anni. Indeed, this is not the only reference to fairy tales in the novel. When he plays his instrument in the back yards of tenement houses, Andreas is showered with coins from the apartments above, a scene reminiscent of the Grimm Brothers' fairy tale of 'Die Sterntaler' ('The Star Talers', 1812), in which a virtuous girl is rewarded for her charity by silver coins raining down from the heavens. The image painted on the hurdy-gurdy is like the flip side of this fairy tale: in a world of miracles, it suggests, there are also darker forces at play.

In the end, it is not a witch but a much more banal figure who brings about the protagonist's own downfall and transformation. The build-up to the fateful clash on the tram is lengthy, as we are introduced to Herr Arnold's personal affairs, his desire for his secretary, and the unpleasant confrontation with her litigious fiancé. At this point in the novel, we lose sight of Andreas. When he reappears in the following chapter, his sudden outburst of rage is startling; this response is incomprehensible to Pum himself, and yet within the wider context of the novel, it is only too understandable. Not only does this outburst mirror his earlier tremor when faced with the medical commission, it also feeds from his barely disguised mistrust of both authority figures and his fellow citizens. More immediately, though, his response is provoked by a specific accusation made by Herr Arnold and echoed by the crowd of onlookers, who call Andreas 'A simulant! A Bolshevik! A Russian! A spy!' and, finally, 'a Jew' – all of them bywords for the 'other' of the bourgeois order which Andreas himself has made a point of despising. When he is asked for his papers, he refuses and his rage escalates into physical violence: 'Andreas blindly started striking out with his stick. He couldn't see a thing; red flames were circling in front of his eyes.' The scene recalls his medical examination, in which the sight of the blond officer likewise begins to blur in front his eyes. In both scenes, Andreas loses his self-control. His professed faith in the system belies a deeper fear of punishment and humiliation. As he shouts abuse at Herr Arnold, Andreas

had no idea where that cry had come from. Never in his life had he shouted like that; even five minutes earlier it wouldn't have crossed his mind that he would assault a complete stranger and a gentleman in this way. An inexplicable hatred had its way with Andreas. Perhaps it had been in him a long time, buried beneath humility and respect.

Having given us a psychological explanation for Andreas's rage, the narrative also focuses on the role of Herr Arnold in this development, reassuring us that he did not act out of malice but

compelled by a blind Fate to be a hapless tool in the hand of the devil, who on occasion, all unbeknown to us, comes between ourselves and the Almighty; so that we are still sending our prayers up to Him in the comforting certainty that He is there, watching over us – and are astonished not to be heard by Him.

Here, the text returns to the religious model of good – and evil – forces preferred by Pum himself. Indeed, the classical question how evil can prevail in a world governed by a good and powerful God (the problem of theodicy) will come to dominate the second half of the novel, where Andreas's faith in God and an equally benevolent state are undone in the course of his mistreatment and suffering. If the first six chapters chart an upward curve, this direction is radically reversed as Andreas loses first his wife and then his freedom and dignity.

This kind of storyline was not unusual for the time. On the contrary, reflecting the recent social and political upheavals, Weimar culture abounded with tales of social decline, featuring respectable people who fall on hard times. Hans Fallada's novel *Kleiner Mann – was nun?* (*Little Man, What Now?*, 1930) is one prominent example; another is F. W. Murnau's silent film classic *Der letzte Mann* (English title *The Last Laugh*), released in 1924, which tells the story of a hotel doorman who is forced to work as a lavatory attendant and who conceals his new lowly position from his family. Both Fallada's novel and Murnau's film end on a happy note; in the latter, a dying customer leaves the doorman his fortune, so he can return to, and indeed exceed, the comfort and status of his old life. Roth's novel, which was serialized only a few months earlier, closely resembles Murnau's tale even down to the great importance placed on uniforms as symbols of masculine authority, but its conclusion is very different. Where Murnau's doorman emerges with his identity largely unchanged, *Rebellion* is a story of humiliation and eventual death, but also of (spiritual) transformation and rebirth. The novel's final chapters are externally uneventful; what counts is the protagonist's inner life, his reflections and gradual change.

In the chapter following the tram episode, Andreas, having been abandoned by his wife, seeks shelter in Mooli's stable, where he thinks about his life so far and tries to identify any sins which might have brought about his punishment. His soul-searching does not lead to any results; it is only later, during his prison sentence, that he confronts his former self. Here, he begins to speak to the sparrows outside his window, apologizing to them (and all creatures) for his previous indifference:

My dear little birds, for decades you were nothing to me, and I was as indifferent to you as I was to the yellow horse dung in the middle of the streets that was your sustenance. I heard your twittering, of course, but it might have been the buzzing of the bees for all I cared. I didn't know you could feel hunger. I barely knew that people, my own species, could feel hunger. I barely knew what pain was, even though I fought in the War, and lost one leg at the knee. Perhaps I wasn't truly human. Or perhaps my heart was sleeping, and I was sick. That happens. The heart is asleep, it ticks and tocks, but in all other respects it might as well be dead. My poor brain had no thoughts of its own. Nature hasn't blessed me with sharp wits, and my feeble intellect was betrayed by my parents, my school, my teachers, the Sergeant Major and the Captain, and the newspapers I was given to read.

In this central monologue, Andreas comes close to admitting what the war has done to him, namely to deprive him of his humanity. That said, the war is not the only cause behind his inner numbness, for his (self-)critique is also aimed at the social institutions, including school, the army and the family, as well as the media, all of which have contributed to his warped state of mind, making him immune to the suffering of others. His emotional transformation, as we have seen, already started during his marriage to Katharina; during his prison sentence, Andreas builds on this by developing his new affinity with animals – who mirror his own, downtrodden state – but also with other human beings, particularly social outcasts. After his release he sees some burglars breaking into a shop, and yet he does not call the police but lets them get on with their work – a sign of the radical change he has undergone.

But this change goes deeper than bourgeois notions of morality, for it also affects Andreas's faith. In his old world view, social and divine authorities were practically synonymous, but after his arrest Andreas directs his rage and rebellion at God. Having discovered the sparrows outside his prison window, he makes an application to be allowed to feed them, which is declined. Indeed, the guard responds to his request with incomprehension.

'I feel so sorry for the little birdies!' said Andreas, with such a tremulous voice that the guard began to think he had truly lost his mind.

'Don't be ridiculous!' he said. 'God will look after the birds. You'd do better to eat your ration yourself!'

'Do you think?' said Andreas. 'Are you so certain that God will look after them?'

This dialogue alludes to the Sermon on the Mount (Matthew 6:25–33), in which Christ speaks of God's loving care and provision for all His creatures, including the 'birds of the air' and the 'lilies of the field'. Roth's protagonist challenges this biblical image of a good and providential God. The first point on this journey occurs after his release from police custody, an experience which causes him to radically reassess his entire world view: 'When Andreas set foot on the street outside, he felt the world had been freshly painted and renovated, he no longer felt at home in it; just as you feel like a stranger when you return to your room and it's been painted a different color.' It is in this new, detached and clear-sighted state that he loses his faith in a benign God:

Andreas rolled his eyes heavenward, because he wanted to get away from the madness of the world. For Heaven is of a clear and imperishable blue, its color is as pure as divine wisdom, and the clouds forever pass in front of it. But today the clouds formed distorted faces, gargoyles blew by, God was pulling faces.

This passage recalls a scene from Georg Büchner's biographical novella *Lenz* (1836), whose writer-protagonist loses his faith along with sanity. Having tried in vain to raise a young girl from the dead, Lenz looks up, but

the sky was a stupid blue eye, the moon hanging there ridiculously, like an idiot. Lenz was forced to laugh out loud, and with his laughter atheism took hold of him, filling him with calm and solid conviction.*

---

* Georg Büchner, *The Complete Plays*, ed., trans. and intro. Michael Patterson (London: Methuen, 1994), p. 264.

Lenz and Pum are connected by their rage and despair, and yet while for Lenz, heaven is empty, Andreas Pum's position is not that of an atheist but of a man who remains tied to a God he has learned to despise.

Andreas resigns himself to his situation and even finds a kind of contentment while in prison: it is only when he is released that he realizes how much he has lost. On the train back into town, he looks at his face in the lavatory mirror:

Andreas stepped in, and straightway recoiled. There, looking back at him from the narrow mirror facing the door, was an old man with a white beard and a yellow, wrinkled face. The old man reminded him of evil magicians in fairy tales, who command fear and respect . . . Andreas thought he could remember the color of his eyes: had they not once been blue? Now they sparkled with green malignity. Does prison air affect the color of one's eyes?

In yet another reference to the world of fairy tales, Andreas finds himself transformed into an evil magician, and yet in reality his transformed appearance is the result not of some kind of spell but of a merciless penal system. That said, his changed appearance belies his inner transformation into a kinder, more compassionate person; contrary to what he used to believe, appearances do not necessarily reflect someone's inner, moral state.

Though he was only in prison for five weeks, 45-year-old Andreas Pum thus emerges from it an old and broken man. He is discharged one week early, in February or March 1920, having only married Katharina Blumich a few months ago, in November. By charting his rapid ascent and decline, Roth stretches the reader's credulity, and indeed, the reference to fairy tales and magicians alludes to this break with realist convention. Indeed, this moment in the novel is reminiscent of a cinematic montage sequence. But the mirror episode also recalls an earlier, corresponding scene in chapter four where Pum visits the barber to get himself spruced up for Katharina:

He beheld himself in the mirror, his face white with powder, his parting glistening with ointment, and with pride and satisfaction he breathed in the spicy aroma he gave off . . . He flexed his scalp and his forehead, and produced the two impressive little wrinkles either side of his nose, thereby creating the aquiline expression that he had always put on at decisive points in his military career.

Put side by side, these two portraits of the protagonist reveal the destructive power of the state and of the narrative, but also Andreas's earlier attachment to a clichéd model of masculinity. In other regards, however, the novel has a cyclical shape. After his release, Andreas is taken in by Willi, his layabout roommate from before his marriage. When Andreas meets him again, the tables have turned. A former crook, Willi has reinvented himself as a respectable businessman who runs a team of cloakroom and lavatory attendants. Willi's ascent contradicts Andreas's earlier world view and illustrates the fundamental arbitrariness of both success and failure; it also points to a society which is deceived by surfaces and beholden to a certain kind of male charismatic authority.

Willi allows Andreas to stay in his old apartment (which he himself has by now vacated) and hires him as one of his attendants. In this role, Andreas finds another animal friend, namely the parrot Ignatz, who keeps him company at work, and whom he also takes home with him in the evening. He gets to wear his old organ-player uniform, and though his iron cross was stolen in police custody, Willi buys him some new medals in a second-hand shop, asserting that Andreas 'couldn't work in a toilet' without some kind of military decoration. Attired in this way, he carries out his new work in a state of growing detachment, as 'death cast its great blue shadow over Andreas'. Following a narrative sleight of hand, whereby we are simply told that a 'gentleman called for soap' and that Andreas 'didn't hear', the nineteenth and final chapter is a dreamlike epilogue which is once again set in a court room.

The scene starts out in a realist manner, harking back to the court summons which Andreas had received the previous day. And yet as it unfolds, the court room morphs into the tiled washroom where Andreas used to work, and gradually he realizes that he has in fact died. This, then, is not a hearing to review his case and address any miscarriage of justice, but the Last Judgment. Confronting the benevolent-looking judge, Andreas gives an impassioned speech worthy of a tragic hero, in which he accuses God of ignoring human and animal suffering and allowing an unjust world to flourish.

You spawn millions like me in Your senseless fertility, and they grow up, credulous and bowed, they suffer blows in Your name, they salute Emperors, Kings, and Governments in Your name, they suffer purulent wounds of bullets in their bodies, and let three-edged bayonets drill their hearts, or they sink under the yoke of Your industrious days, sour Sundays cheaply frame their brutal weeks, they are hungry and silent, their children wither, their wives grow ugly and unfaithful, the laws proliferate across their path like treacherous creepers, their feet are ensnared in the tangle of Your edicts, they fall and pray to You, and You do not raise them up.

This, his closing monologue, is the climax of the novel; its high tone evokes the psalms of the Old Testament but with an inverse, accusatory inflection. Indeed, six years later, Roth published his great novel *Hiob* (*Job*, 1930), which he modelled on the biblical narrative. But where its protagonist overcomes his tribulations with his faith restored, *Rebellion* offers no such consolation. Andreas Pum does not find redemption after death, but nor is he able to simply abnegate God. Though he refuses God's mercy and asks to be sent to hell, he is asked whether he wants to be a museum guard, a park attendant or to run a tobacco shop – his three ambitions from the first chapter. The donkey Mooli, who had been sold by Katharina and led away in a heart-wrenching scene, also reappears in this dying scene:

Then all at once, Mooli, the little donkey, appeared next to Andreas, pulling the hurdy-gurdy, which was playing even without anyone to crank its handle. Ignatz the parrot perched on Andreas's shoulder. The judge stood up, he loomed bigger and bigger, his gray countenance began to shine white, his red lips parted in a smile. Andreas began to cry. He didn't know if he was in Heaven or Hell.

The novel thus ends on a note of nihilistic uncertainty; back in real life, however, it closes with bathetic understatement. After his death, Andreas's body is donated to science, to be cut up even further by yet another faceless institution. Willi visits the body at the Anatomical Institute before it is dissected: 'He was on the point of tears when he remembered the tune he always liked to whistle'.

Roth's novel is a searing critique of inter-war society as seen through the eyes of one who, having regarded himself as part of the status quo, ends up rejecting both the worldly order and the divine. On some level, the persistent association of God and government may seem anachronistic, a fall-back to a much older view of the world, but Roth uses it to trace Pum's radical journey from certainty to nihilism. On this journey, rage and rebellion give rise to a new sense of compassion; and even as he slumps into resignation, Andreas retains his new-found affinity with children, social outcasts, and animals. In this way, Roth's protagonist gains his humanity precisely as humanity rejects him.

Carolin Duttlinger

CAROLIN DUTTLINGER is Professor of German Literature and Culture at the University of Oxford and Fellow and Tutor in German at Wadham College, Oxford.

SELECT BIBLIOGRAPHY

ACOCELLA, JOAN, 'European Dreams: Rediscovering Joseph Roth', *New Yorker*, 19 January 2004, 81–86.

CHAMBERS, HELEN, 'Signs of the Times: Joseph Roth's Weimar Journalism', in *German Novelists of the Weimar Republic: Intersections of Literature and Politics*, ed. Karl Leydecker (Rochester, NY: Camden House, 2006).

COETZEE, J. M., 'Emperor of Nostalgia', *The New York Review of Books*, 28 February 2002.

HUGHES, JON, *Facing Modernity: Fragmentation, Culture, and Identity in Joseph Roth's Writing in the 1920s* (London: Maney, 2006).

LAZAROMS, ILSE JOSEPHA, *The Grace of Misery: Joseph Roth and the Politics of Exile, 1919–1939* (Leiden: Brill, 2012).

KEEL, DANIEL and DANIEL KAMPA (eds), *Joseph Roth: Leben und Werk* (Zurich: Diogenes, 2010).

ROBERTSON, RITCHIE, 'Austrian Prose Fiction, 1918–45', in *A History of Austrian Literature 1918–2000*, ed. Katrin Kohl and Ritchie Robertson (Rochester, NY: Camden House, 2006), pp. 53–74.

TONKIN, KATI, *Joseph Roth's March into History: From the Early Novels to 'Radetzkymarsch' and 'Die Kapuzinergruft'* (Rochester, NY: Camden House, 2008).

CHRONOLOGY

DATE	AUTHOR'S LIFE	LITERARY CONTEXT
1894	Born (2 September) in Brody, Austrian Galicia, of Jewish parents. As a boy, Roth lived in his grandfather's house in Brody with his mother after the father was committed to an asylum; spent summer holidays with an uncle (mother's brother) in Lemberg.	Rilke: *Leben und Lieder.* H. Mann: *In einer Familie.* Schnitzler: *Das Märchen.* Hamsun: *Pan.* Kipling: *The Jungle Book.*
1895		Fontane: *Effi Briest.* Schnitzler: *Light-o'-Love.* Wedekind: *Earth Spirit.* Crane: *The Red Badge of Courage.*
1896		Altenberg: *Wie ich es sehe.* Fontane: *Die Poggenpuhls.* Sudermann: *Morituri.* Chekhov: *The Seagull.*
1897		Rilke: *Traumgekrönt.* Strindberg: *Inferno.*
1898		Schnitzler: *Die Frau des Weisen.* T. Mann: *Little Herr Friedemann.* Pontoppidan: *Lucky Per* (to 1904).
1899		Zola: *J'accuse.* Rilke: *Mir zur Feier.* Schnitzler: *Leutnant Gustl*; *Frau Berta Gartan.* Hauptmann: *Fuhrmann Henschel.* Fontane: *Der Stechlin.* Tolstoy: *Resurrection.* Ibsen: *When We Dead Awaken.* James: *The Awkward Age.*
1900	Attends Jewish community school in Brody (to 1905).	Schnitzler: *Reigen.*
1901		T. Mann: *Buddenbrooks.* Strindberg: *Dance of Death.* Chekhov: *Three Sisters.*
1902		Wedekind: *Pandora's Box.* Rilke: *The Book of Pictures.* Gide: *L'Immoraliste.* James: *The Wings of the Dove.*

HISTORICAL EVENTS

Franz Joseph I Austrian Emperor since 1848. Dreyfus trial begins in France. Resignation of Gladstone in Britain. Death of Alexander III in Russia; accession of Nicholas II.

Lumière brothers invent cinematograph. Marconi invents wireless telegraphy. Freud's *Studien über Hysterie* inaugurates psychoanalysis. X-rays discovered (Röntgen).

Wilhelm II announces German pursuit of 'world politics'. Theodor Herzl, founder of modern political Zionism, publishes *Der Judenstaat*, putting forward the idea of a Jewish national home in Palestine.

Assassination of Elisabeth, wife of Franz Joesph I, in Geneva. First Zionist Congress in Basel. Vienna *Sezession* led by painter Gustav Klimt and architect Otto Wagner, to further modern (*Jugendstil*) movement. German Navy Law begins the arms race. Death of Bismarck. Curies discover radium.

Renewal of *Ausgleich* of 1867 (established Dual Monarchy of Austria–Hungary) following agitation for its repeal and (in 1897) breakdown in constitutional government and rule by Imperial decree. *Die Fackel* (edited by Karl Kraus) founded. Berlin *Sezession* founded by *avant-garde* artists under Max Liebermann. Schoenberg. *Verklärte Nacht.*

Beginning of severe recession in Austria–Hungary (to 1907). Bülow Chancellor of Germany. Freud: *The Interpretation of Dreams.* First Zeppelin. Death of Queen Victoria; accession of Edward VII. Roosevelt US President after McKinley's assassination. First wireless communication between Europe and US. Picasso's 'blue period' (to 1904). Triple Alliance (Germany, Austria, Italy) renewed to 1914. Klimt's revolutionary *Beethovenfries* at the Vienna *Sezession* Exhibition.

xxv

DATE	AUTHOR'S LIFE	LITERARY CONTEXT
1903		T. Mann: *Tristan*; *Tonio Kröger*.
		Hauptmann: *Rosa Bernd*.
		Shaw: *Man and Superman*.
		Butler: *The Way of all Flesh*.
		James: *The Ambassadors*.
1904		Hofmannsthal: *Elektra*.
		Pirandello: *The Late Mattia Pascal*.
		Conrad: *Nostromo*.
1905	Attends grammar school in Brody (to 1913).	Rilke: *The Book of Hours*.
		H. Mann: *Professor Unrat*.
1906		Hofmannsthal: *Oepidus and the Sphinx*.
		Wedekind: *Spring Awakening*.
		Musil: *Young Törless*.
		Galsworthy: *The Man of Property*.
1907		Rilke: *New Poems* (to 1908).
		Strindberg: *The Ghost Sonata*.
		Conrad. *The Secret Agent*.
1908		Altenberg: *Märchen des Lebens*.
		Schnitzler: *Der Weg ins Freie*.
		Maeterlinck: *L'Oiseau bleu*.
1909		Rilke: *Requiem*.
		H. Mann: *Die kleine Stadt*.
		Bely: *The Silver Dove*.
		Gide: *La Porte étroite*.
1910	Death of father who had been insane since before Roth's birth.	Rilke: *Sketches of Malte Laurids Brigge*.
		Forster: *Howards End*.
1911		Altenberg: *Neues Altes*.
		Hauptmann: *Die Ratten*.
		Conrad: *Under Western Eyes*.
		Pound: *Canzoni*.
1912		T. Mann: *Death in Venice*.
		Kafka: *Amerika*.
		Hesse: *Rosshalde*.
		Hofmannsthal: *Everyman*.
		Pound: *Ripostes*.
1913	Gains school-leaving certificate with distinction. Enrols at University of Lemberg (winter semester).	Trakl: *Gedichte*.
		Alain Fournier: *Le Grand Meaulnes*.
		Proust: *Remembrance of Things Past* (to 1927).
		Gorky: *Childhood*.
		Lawrence: *Sons and Lovers*.

xxvi

CHRONOLOGY

HISTORICAL EVENTS

King Alexander of Serbia and Queen Draga murdered. Austria–Hungary and Russia agree on respective rights in south-east Europe. Conflict between Bolsheviks and Mensheviks at Congress of Russian Social Democratic Party. First flight by Wright brothers.

Russo-Japanese War. *Entente cordiale* between Britain and France. *Die Brücke* group of artists formed in Dresden.

First Russian Revolution. 'Red Sunday' in St Petersburg. Beginning of Fauvism. Einstein's Special Theory of Relativity. Richard Strauss: *Salome*. Constitution in Russia: first Duma meets and is speedily dissolved. Charges against Dreyfus finally quashed.

Ausgleich again renewed. Universal suffrage in Austria–Hungary. Triple Entente (Britain, France, Russia). Hague Peace Conference fails to halt arms race.

Austria annexes Bosnia and Herzegovina. Schoenberg arrives at atonality with his *Three Piano Pieces*. Cubist movement. Klimt: *The Kiss*. Mahler: *The Song of the Earth*.

Zionists found Tel Aviv. Blériot flies English Channel. Gide and others establish *Nouvelle Revue Française*. *Der Neue Club* formed in Berlin. Futurist movement founded by Italian poet Marinetti. Matisse: *The Dance*.

Death of Edward VII; accession of George V. First London Post-Impressionist exhibition. Herwarth Walden founds periodical *Der Sturm*.

Amundsen reaches South Pole. Strauss/Hofmannstahl: *Der Rosenkavalier*. Death of Mahler. *Der Blaue Reiter* founded in Berlin.

Balkan League formed (Serbia, Bulgaria, Montenegro). Diets suppressed throughout Empire following serious disorder in Croatia. Sinking of the *Titanic*. Schoenberg: *Pierre Lunaire*. Strauss/Hofmannsthal: *Ariadne auf Naxos*.

Treaty of London ends first Balkan War. Second Balkan War (June–August). Treaty of Bucharest: partitioning of the Balkans. Einstein's General Theory of Relativity. Freud: *Totem and Taboo*.

REBELLION

DATE	AUTHOR'S LIFE	LITERARY CONTEXT
1914	Enrols at University of Vienna and studies German literature.	Rilke: *Fünf Gesänge*. Bahr: *Expressionism*. Joyce: *Dubliners*; *A Portrait of the Artist as a Young Man* (to 1915).
1915		H. Mann: *Emile Zola*. Kafka: *Metamorphosis*. Ford: *The Good Soldier*.
1916	Volunteers in Austrian rifle regiment.	Brod: *Tycho Brahes Weg zu Gott*. Bahr: *Himmelfahrt*. Barbusse: *Under Fire*.
1917	Is sent to the army press office in Galicia.	Eliot: *Prufrock and other Observations*. Pound: *Cantos 1–3*.
1918	Back in Vienna during December; then returns east, becoming involved in the Czech–Ukrainian war.	Altenberg: *Vita ipsa*. Kaiser: *Gas*. Kraus: *The Last Days of Mankind*. H. Mann: *Der Untertan* (1st of *Kaiserreich* trilogy). T. Mann: *Reflections of an Unpolitical Man*. Spengler: *The Decline of the West*.
1919	Returns to Vienna, taking up journalism.	Altenberg: *Mein Lebensabend*. Dos Passos: *One Man's Initiation*. Hesse: *Demian*. Kafka: *A Country Doctor*.
1920	Moves to Berlin.	Döblin: *Wallenstein*. Zamyatin: *We*. S. Zweig: *Drei Meister*. Lawrence: *Women in Love*. Wharton: *The Age of Innocence*.
1921		Hašek: *The Good Soldier Švejk*. Hofmannsthal: *The Difficult Man*. Pirandello: *Six Characters in Search of an Author*. Dos Passos: *Three Soldiers*.
1922	Marries Friederike Reichler.	Brecht: *Baal*; *Drums in the Night*. S. Zweig: *Amok*. Hesse: *Siddhartha*. Bely: *Petersburg*. Valéry: *Charmes*. Eliot: *The Waste Land*. Joyce: *Ulysses*. Woolf: *Jacob's Room*.

CHRONOLOGY

HISTORICAL EVENTS

Heir to Austro-Hungarian throne, Archduke Franz Ferdinand d'Este and his wife, Sophie, assassinated in Sarajevo (June). Austria–Hungary declares war on Serbia (July). World War I breaks out (August). Austrian armies suffer heavy defeats (1914–15) when Russia invades Galicia. President Wilson proclaims US neutrality.
Serbia and Poland overrun by Austro-Hungarian and German troops. Entry of Italy into the war. Heavy fighting at Gallipoli. Sinking of the *Lusitania*.

Death of Emperor Franz Joseph; accession of Charles I. Murder of Austrian premier Stürgh; growing unpopularity of war leads to rioting. Tzara founds Dada movement in Zürich. Jung: *The Psychology of the Unconscious*.
US enters war on Allied side. February Revolution in Russia; fall of monarchy. Lenin's return to Russia; October (Bolshevik) Revolution. Italians defeated by Austrian army at Caporetto (October). Balfour Declaration promises a Jewish homeland in Palestine. Freud: *Introductory Lectures*.
Wilson's Fourteen Points (January); point 10 includes notion of self-determination for the nationalities of Austria–Hungary. Russia signs peace of Brest-Litovsk with Germany and Austria–Hungary (March). Italian troops overwhelm Austrian forces (October). Allies occupy Constantinople. End of World War I (November). Collapse of Austrian Empire; abdication of Charles I; Austrian republic declared, with Renner (Social Democrat) as first Chancellor (to 1920). Balkan countries declare independence. Abdication of Wilhelm II in Germany. Assassination of Nicholas II in Russia. Russian Civil War (to 1921). Grosz: *Fit for Active Service*.
Treaty of Versailles. Treaty of Saint-Germain dissolves Habsburg Empire and defines Austria's borders. Great Austrian inflation (to 1923). Weimar Republic constituted; a 'Soviet Republic' established in Munich and swiftly repressed. Bauhaus founded by Walter Gropius. Rutherford splits the atom.
New Austrian constitution. Struggle between Social Democrats and Christian Socialists dominates Austrian politics. Social Democrats remain dominant in 'Red Vienna' until 1934, their achievements, particularly in municipal housing, internationally acclaimed. The Kapp *putsch* defeated by Berlin workers. First meeting of League of Nations. Irish Civil War. Prohibition in US. Wiene directs Expressionist film *The Cabinet of Dr Caligari*.
New Economic Policy in Russia. Rise of Fascism in Italy. Schoenberg's Suite Op. 25, his first work wholly in the 12-note method. Serialist composers Webern and Berg also working in Vienna at this time.

Mussolini's march on Rome; Italian Fascists come to power. USSR founded. Stalin General Secretary of Russian Communist Party Central Committee. Ottoman Empire dissolved. In Germany, political assassinations of Erzberger and Rathenau by right-wing extremists. Max Weber: *Economy and Society*. Wittgenstein: *Tractatus Logico-Philosophicus*.

DATE	AUTHOR'S LIFE	LITERARY CONTEXT
1923	*Das Spinnennetz* (*The Spider's Web*).	Rilke: *Sonnets to Orpheus*; *Duino Elegies*. T. Mann: *Von deutscher Republik*. Toller: *Der deutsche Hinkemann*. Svevo: *The Confessions of Zeno*. Gorky: *My Universities*.
1924	*Hotel Savoy*; *Die Rebellion*.	T. Mann: *The Magic Mountain*. Musil: *Drei Frauen*. Trotsky: *Literature and Revolution*. Ford: *Parade's End* (to 1928).
1925	In Paris as correspondent of the *Frankfurter Zeitung*.	Kafka: *The Trial*. S. Zweig: *Volpone*. Zuckmayer: *Der fröhliche Weinberg*. Bulgakov: *The White Guard*. Fitzgerald: *The Great Gatsby*.
1926	Visits Soviet Union, after loss of Paris post.	Kafka: *The Castle*. Brecht: *Mann ist Mann*. Schnitzler: *Traumnovelle*. Babel: *Red Cavalry*.
1927	Leaves *Frankfurter Zeitung* where he worked as reporter, then editor. *Die Flucht ohne Ende* (*Flight Without End*); *Juden auf Wanderschaft* (essays).	Hesse: *Der Steppenwolf*. A. Zweig: *The Case of Sergeant Grischa*. S. Zweig: *Verwirrung der Gefühle*. Brod: *Eine Frau, nach der man sich sehnt*. Woolf: *To the Lighthouse*.
1928	*Zipper und sein Vater* – heralds his success as a novelist. Beginning of his wife's schizophrenia.	Hofmannsthal: *The Tower*. H. Mann: *Eugénie oder Die Bürgerzeit*. Nabokov: *King, Queen, Knave*. Sholokhov: *And Quiet Flows the Don* (to 1940). Waugh: *Decline and Fall*.
1929	*Der Stumme Prophet* (*The Silent Prophet*); *Rechts und Links* (*Right and Left*). Meets Andrea Manga Bell. Works for Munich paper (to 1930).	Remarque: *All Quiet on the Western Front*. Döblin: *Berlin Alexanderplatz*. Kraus: *Literatur und Lüge*. Faulkner: *The Sound and the Fury*. Hemingway: *A Farewell to Arms*. Graves: *Goodbye to All That*.

CHRONOLOGY

HISTORICAL EVENTS

Failure of Hitler's Munich *putsch*. French occupy Ruhr. Rampant inflation in Germany. In Austria, years of economic instability, poverty and unemployment give rise to extremist groups, both leftist and Pan-German (Nazi). Le Corbusier: *Towards a New Architecture*. Dix: *The Trench*.

Death of Lenin. First Labour government in Britain under Ramsay MacDonald. André Breton: Surrealist Manifesto.

Hindenburg elected as second Chancellor of German Republic, in succession to Ebert. Berg: *Wozzek*. Eisenstein: *The Battleship Potemkin*. Hitler: *Mein Kampf*.

General strike in Britain. Germany admitted to League of Nations.

Social Democrat riots in Vienna following acquittal of Nazis for political murder. Formation of *Heimwehr*, or bourgeois private army, to challenge the activities of Socialists' illegal armed bands. Trotsky expelled from Russian Communist Party. Lindbergh flies Atlantic solo.

Stalin de facto dictator in USSR: first Five Year Plan. Brecht/Weill: *Threepenny Opera*. Heidegger: *Time and Being*. Discovery of penicillin by A. Fleming.

Wall Street Crash: world economics crisis. Stalin's collectivization of agriculture of USSR begins.

DATE	AUTHOR'S LIFE	LITERARY CONTEXT
1930	*Hiob* (*Job*); *Panoptikum* (essays). *Die Flucht ohne Ende* (*Flight Without End*) published in English translation by Hutchinson (UK) and Doubleday (US).	T. Mann: *Mario and the Magician*; *Die Forderung des Tages*. Hesse: *Narziss and Goldmund*. Musil: *The Man without Qualities*. Sudermann: *The Dance of Youth*.
1931		H. Mann: *Geist und Tat*. Zuckmayer: *The Captain of Köpenick*. Horváth: *Tales from the Vienna Woods*.
1932	*Radetzkymarsch* (*The Radetzky March*).	Broch: *The Sleepwalkers*. Hesse: *Morgenlandfahrt*. Huxley: *Brave New World*. Céline: *Journey to the End of the Night*.
1933	Roth's work burnt by Nazis. Emigrates to Paris: works on journals and newspapers for exiles.	T. Mann: *The Tales of Jakob* (first of *Joseph* tetralogy). Lorca: *Blood Wedding*.
1934	Lives in South of France (to June 1935).	Broch: *The Unknown Quantity*. Weinheber: *Adel und Untergang*. Bánffy: *The Transylvanian Trilogy* (to 1940). Laxness: *Independent People*. Fitzgerald: *Tender is the Night*.
1935	*Die Büste des Kaisers*; *Tarabas, ein Gast auf dieser Erde* (*Tarabas: A Guest on Earth*). Returns to Paris.	Klausmann: *Symphonie pathétique*. H. Mann: *Die Jugend des Königs Henri Quatre* (2nd vol. 1938). Brecht: *Furcht und Elend des Dritten Reiches* (to 1938). Döblin: *Pardon wird nicht gegeben*. Canetti: *Auto da Fé*.
1936	*Die hundert Tage*; *Beichte eines Mörders*. Amsterdam (March–June), Ostend (July), Paris (late 1936).	K. Mann: *Mephisto*. H. Mann: *Es kommt der Tag*. Lorca: *La Casa de Bernarda Alba*. Faulkner: *Absalom, Absalom!*
1937	*Das falsche Gewicht* (*Weights and Measures*). Travels to Poland, stays in Vienna. Paris again.	Brecht: *The Life of Galileo* (to 1939). Nabokov: *The Gift*. Hemingway: *To Have and Have Not*.

CHRONOLOGY

HISTORICAL EVENTS

In Austria Social Democrats replace Christian Socialists as largest single party but are still obliged to rely for support on the pan-German groups. Freud: *Civilization and its Discontents*. Brecht/Weill: *Aufstieg und Fall der Stadt Mahagonny*.

Austrian customs union with Germany; failure of largest bank in Austria. Collapse of government. Christian Socialists returned to power and customs union renounced.

Roosevelt President of the US: New Deal. Dollfuss becomes Austrian Chancellor; allies with *Heimwehr* group and pursues a line independent from both pan-Germans and Socialists, antagonizing both. First autobahn, Cologne–Bonn, opened.

In Germany, Nazis under Hitler come to power by constitutional means but swiftly establish one-party state with violent suppression of opponents; beginning of the Third Reich. Jung: *Modern Man in Search of a Soul*.

Socialists rise against *Heimwehr*; for one week Vienna and other Austrian cities in state of civil war. Rebels crushed and leaders executed. Dollfuss murdered. Succeeded by Schuschnigg. Stringent laws against political violence; under new constitution Austrian independence effectively surrendered to Germany.

Nuremberg Laws depriving Jews in Germany of citizenship. Italy invades Abyssinia. Berg: *Lulu*.

Outbreak of Spanish Civil War. Abdication of Edward VIII in Britain. Stalin's Great Purges in Russia (to 1938).

Religious persecution in Germany. Rome–Berlin axis formed. Japanese invade China. Orff: *Carmina Burana*.

xxxiii

DATE	AUTHOR'S LIFE	LITERARY CONTEXT
1938	*Die Kapuzinergruft* (*The Capuchin Crypt*). Last visit to Vienna; last visit to Amsterdam. Declining health.	Beckett: *Murphy*. Sartre: *Nausea*.
1939	*Die Legende von heiligen Trinker*; *Die Geschichte der 1002. Nacht.* Dies as a result of alcoholism (May).	T. Mann: *Lotte in Weimar*. S. Zweig: *Beware of Pity*. Joyce: *Finnegans Wake*. Isherwood: *Goodbye to Berlin*. Steinbeck: *The Grapes of Wrath*.

CHRONOLOGY

HISTORICAL EVENTS

Hitler's *Anschluss* (annexation of Austria). *Kristallnacht* in Germany.
Munich Crisis.

Franco's Nationalists victorious in Spain. Soviet–German Pact. Germany
occupies parts of Czechoslovakia; attacks Poland, ignores Anglo-French
ultimatum. Beginning of World War II.

REBELLION

Chapter 1

THE 24TH MILITARY HOSPITAL was a cluster of shacks on the edge of the city. It would have taken an able-bodied man a good half hour's walk to reach it from the end of the tramline. The tram went into the world, the big city and life. But to the inmates of the 24th Military Hospital the tram was out of reach.

They were blind or halt. They limped. They had shattered spines. They were waiting to have limbs amputated, or had recently had them amputated. The War was in the dim and distant past. They had forgotten about squad drill, about the Sergeant Major, the Captain, the Company, the Chaplain, the Emperor's birthday, the parade, the trenches, going over the top. They had made their own individual peace with the enemy. Now they were readying themselves for the next war: against pain, against artificial limbs, against crippledom, against hunchbacks, against sleepless nights, and against the healthy and the hale.

Only Andreas Pum was content with things as they were. He had lost a leg and been given a medal. There were many who had no medal, even though they had lost more than merely a leg. They had lost both arms or both legs. Or they would be bedridden for the rest of their lives, because there was something the matter with their spinal fluid. Andreas Pum rejoiced when he saw the sufferings of the others.

He believed in a just god. One who handed out shrapnel, amputations, and medals to the deserving. Viewed in the correct light, the loss of a leg wasn't so very bad, and the joy of receiving a medal was considerable. An invalid might enjoy the respect of the world. An invalid with a medal could depend on that of the government.

The government is something that overlies man like the sky overlies the earth. What comes from it may be good or ill, but it cannot be other than great and all-powerful, unknowable and mysterious, even though on occasion it may be understood by an ordinary person.

Some of his comrades curse at the government. According to them, they have been treated unjustly. As if the War hadn't been a necessity! As if its consequences were not inevitably pain, amputations, hunger, and sickness! What were they grumbling about? They had no God, no Emperor, no Fatherland. They were no better than heathens. 'Heathens' is the best term for someone who opposes the determinations of a government.

It was a warm Sunday morning in April, and Andreas Pum was sitting on one of the crude white wooden benches that had been put out on the lawn in front of the hospital shacks. Almost all of the other benches were occupied by two or three convalescents, sitting together and talking. Only Andreas was on his own, rejoicing in the designation he had come up with for his comrades.

They were heathens, no less than people who were sent to prison for perjury, theft, assault, or murder. What possessed people to kill, steal, swindle, and desert? The fact that they were heathens.

If someone had happened to ask Andreas just then what heathens are, he would have replied: criminals who are in prison, or perhaps still at large. Andreas Pum was highly delighted with his notion of 'heathens.' The word satisfied him; it answered his swirling questions and solved many riddles. It absolved him of the necessity of continuing to reflect and to think about the others. Andreas was happy with his word. At the same time, it gave him a feeling of superiority to his comrades chattering away on the other benches. Some of them were more badly hurt and had no medals. Was that unjust? Why were they cursing? Why were they complaining? Were they worried about their future? If they continued to be so obdurate, they really would have every reason to worry. They were digging their own graves! Why should the government look out for its enemies? Himself, though, Andreas Pum, it surely would look out for.

And – while the sun moved briskly and confidently toward its zenith in the cloudless sky, becoming ever more radiant and even a little summery – Andreas Pum contemplated the years ahead. The government will have found him a little postage stamp concession or a place as an attendant in a shady park or a cool museum. So there he sits, with his cross on his chest; soldiers salute him, a passing general gives him a pat on the back, and little children are terrified of him. Not that he does them any harm, he just makes sure they don't go running around on the grass. Or visitors to the museum buy their catalogs and postcards from him, though to them he is not an ordinary tradesman, but more like a kind of state official. It's not beyond possibility that a widow may present herself, childless or maybe with a child, or a spinster. A well-situated invalid with a pension is not a bad match, and after a war men are in short supply.

The jangle of a bell skipped across the lawn in front of the shacks, announcing lunch. The invalids got up with difficulty and staggered, propped up on one another, toward the long wooden refectory building. Andreas swiftly bent down to pick up his crutches, and hobbled away in pursuit of his comrades. He wasn't quite convinced by their pain. He, too, had to suffer. But see how quickly he can move when the lunch bell summons!

Naturally, he overtakes all the halt and the blind, and those men whose shattered spines are so crooked that their backs are parallel to the ground they walk on. They call out after Andreas Pum, but he has no intention of waiting for them.

There was gruel, as there always was on Sundays. The invalids intoned their regular Sunday complaint: gruel is boring. But Andreas didn't find it at all boring. He raised the bowl to his lips and drank it down, having vainly trawled through it with his spoon a couple of times. The others looked on, and hesitantly followed his example. He kept the bowl at his lips a long time, and peered over the edge of it at his comrades. He saw that they liked the gruel, too, and their complaining had been all for show. They're heathens! crowed Andreas to himself, and he put his bowl down.

The dried vegetables, which the others called 'barbed wire,' were less to his liking. Nevertheless, he finished his plate. It gave him the satisfying feeling of having done his duty, as though he had polished up his rusty rifle. He regretted that there was no NCO on hand to inspect the plates. His plate was as clean as his conscience. A sunbeam struck the china, and it gleamed. It looked like a check mark from Heaven.

That afternoon brought the long-awaited visit of Princess Mathilde in a nurse's uniform. Andreas, who was in charge of the ward on his wing, stood at attention in the doorway. The princess shook his hand, and he bowed in spite of himself, for he had resolved to stay at attention. His crutches fell to the ground, and Princess Mathilde's lady-in-waiting stooped to pick them up.

The princess left, followed by the head sister, the head doctor, and the priest. 'Old harlot!' shouted a man from the second row of beds. 'Shut your face!' cried Andreas. The others laughed. Andreas lost his temper. 'Make your beds!' he ordered, even though the blankets were all double-folded, as they had to be. No one moved. One or two even started filling their pipes.

Then Engineer Lang, a private first class, who had lost his right arm and whom Andreas respected, said: 'Don't get all het up, Andreas, we're all poor buggers here!'

The barracks became very quiet; everyone looked at the engineer, as Lang stood in front of Andreas and spoke.

It wasn't clear whether he was addressing Andreas, or all of them, or just talking to himself. He looked out the window and said:

'Princess Mathilde will be very pleased just now. She, too, will have had a hard day. Every Sunday she goes and visits four hospitals. For, as you must know, there are more hospitals than there are princesses, and more sick people than healthy. People who think they're healthy are sick, too, though many of them aren't aware of it. Maybe they'll make peace before long.'

A few cleared their throats. The man from the second row of bunks who had earlier shouted 'Old harlot!' now coughed loudly. Andreas hobbled over to his cot, took a pack of cigarettes off the shelf and called to the engineer. 'A cigarette, Doctor?' He always addressed the engineer as 'Doctor.'

Lang talked like a heathen, but also like a priest. Maybe it was because he was educated. He was always right about everything. You felt like arguing with him, but you couldn't find any grounds for doing so. He had to be right if you couldn't argue with him.

That evening, the engineer lay on his bed fully clothed and said: 'Once the borders are open again, I'll be out of here. There's nothing left for me in Europe.'

'There will be if we win the war,' said Andreas.

'Everyone will lose it,' replied the engineer. Andreas Pum didn't understand what he meant, but he nodded respectfully anyway, as though forced to agree.

He for his part decided to stay in the country and sell picture postcards in a museum. He could see that that might not be a prospect for an educated man. Or was the engineer supposed to become a park attendant as well?

Andreas had no family. When the others had visitors, he went out and read a book from the hospital library. He had at various times thought of marriage. But the fear that he didn't earn enough to feed a family had kept him from asking for the hand of Annie the cook, Amalie the seamstress, or Poldi the governess.

He had only gone out with the three of them. His job didn't suit a young wife either. Andreas worked as a night watchman in a lumberyard outside the city, and only had one night off each week. His jealous nature would have robbed him of his satisfaction in the conscientious performance of his duty, or even made it completely impossible.

A few of the men were asleep and snoring. Engineer Lang was reading. 'Shall I turn the light out?' asked Andreas.

'Yes,' said the engineer, putting his book down.

'Good night, Doctor,' said Andreas. He switched off the light. He got undressed in the dark. He leaned his crutch against the wall to the right of the bed.

Before going to sleep, Andreas thinks of the prosthesis the

head doctor has promised him. It will be a perfect prosthesis, as good as Captain Hainigl's. With him, you wouldn't even know he'd lost a leg. The Captain walks through the room quite unaided, it just looks as though he has one leg longer than the other. Artificial limbs are an enlightened invention, an example of the trouble the government will go to. There's no denying that.

Chapter 2

THE ARTIFICIAL LIMB never came. In its place there came unrest, upheaval, and revolution. Andreas Pum only set his mind at rest two weeks later, after he'd understood from newspapers, the events, and what people said that republics also had governments that steered their destinies just like monarchies. In the great cities the rabble-rousers were shot at. The Spartacist heathens would stop at nothing. They probably wanted to do away with the government altogether. They didn't know what they wanted instead. They were wicked or foolish, they were shot, and it served them right. Ordinary people shouldn't get mixed up in the affairs of clever men.

Meanwhile, Pum and the heathens were waiting for a medical commission. It was to decide on the numbers to live in the hospital, on the patients' ability or inability to work, on provision for the inmates. According to a rumor that fluttered over from other hospitals, only those patients with shell shock would be allowed to remain. Everyone else would be given some money and maybe a license to play the barrel organ. There was no possibility of a postage stamp concession, or a watchman's post in a park or museum.

Andreas began to feel sorry he didn't have shell shock. Among the 156 patients in the 24th Military Hospital, there was only one with shell shock. All the others envied him.

He was a blacksmith by the name of Bossi, of Italian descent, dark, swarthy, broad-shouldered. His hair hung down over his eyes and threatened to cover his whole face, spreading over his narrow forehead, covering his cheeks and joining forces with his heavy beard.

Bossi's condition did nothing to diminish the fearful effect of his brute physicality, but actually made it still more menacing. His low brow beetled and vanished between the bushy eyebrows and the low hairline. His green eyes became more prominent, his beard shook, you could hear his teeth chattering. The colossal legs bent, so that his kneecaps now knocked together, now twisted apart, his shoulders flew up and down, while his massive head was caught in a perpetual gentle shaking of the kind one often sees in the feeble heads of old women. The incessant movements of his body made it impossible for the blacksmith to enunciate clearly. He would burble half a sentence, spit out a word, fall silent, and then begin again. That such a wild-looking, mighty man was condemned to shake made his familiar condition appear yet more terrible than it already was. A great sadness befell everyone who saw the trembling blacksmith. He was like a staggering colossus on uncertain foundations. Everyone expected his imminent collapse, but it never happened. It defied belief that a man of his dimensions could so continually shake without falling and, to the relief of himself and those around him, finally disintegrating. In Bossi's presence, even the most pitiable patients, the ones with shattered spines, were terrified, as if some looming catastrophe were forever waiting to happen.

Anyone who saw him felt at once the desire to help him and a sensation of utter helplessness. It was painful and humiliating to acknowledge that there was nothing you could do. One felt like trembling oneself, from guilt and solidarity. His affliction seemed almost to be contagious. Finally, one withdrew, shrank back, but was still unable to forget the picture of the trembling giant.

Three days before the commission was due, Andreas visited Bossi's barracks, which he had so far strenuously avoided. A score of amputees and cripples were sitting in a ring around the blacksmith, gazing at him in silent compassion. Maybe they hoped to catch his trembling from him. Certainly, now one, now another felt a violent twitching of the knee, the elbow, the wrist. They didn't admit it to each other. One by one, they crept away and practiced their new skill when they had a moment to themselves.

The suspicious Andreas, who for reasons that weren't entirely clear to him disliked Bossi, was at first inclined to doubt his condition. He felt envy, and for the first time a little bitterness toward the government, for its decision to favor those with shell shock and no one else. For the first time, he understood the unfairness of those who were in command and in authority. Suddenly he felt his muscles spasm, his mouth skew, his right eyelid begin to twitch. He felt a joyful pain. He hobbled away. His muscles calmed themselves. His eyelid stopped twitching.

Andreas couldn't sleep. He got dressed in the dark and, without his crutches, so as not to wake the others, propped his hands on the bed head and the table and slid his leg in the direction of the window and his upper body after it. He saw a section of darkened lawn and the gleaming white fence. For over an hour he stood there, thinking about his barrel organ.

It's a bright summer afternoon. Andreas is standing in the courtyard of a large house, in the shadow of a leafy old tree. Perhaps a linden tree. Andreas cranks the handle of his barrel organ and plays 'Once I Had a Comrade' or 'Outside the City

Gate' or the National Anthem. He is in uniform. He is wearing his medal. Coins, wrapped in tissue paper, are flying down from all the open windows. He hears the muffled jingling as they land. There are children there. Housemaids lean out from the windowsills. Careless of the danger. Andreas plays.

The moon rose over the edge of the woods in front of the hospital. It got light. Andreas was afraid his comrades might see him standing there in the gloaming. He slid back to bed.

For the next two days he was quiet and preoccupied.

The commission came. Each patient was summoned to appear individually before it. A man stood by the curtain that shielded the commission from the eyes of the waiting patients. Each time, the man pulled back the curtain and called out a name. Each time, a frail body left the ranks of the others and swayed, tottered, or limped behind the curtain. The individuals didn't come back once they had been examined. They left the room by a different exit. They were issued a piece of paper, went back to their shacks, packed their belongings, and crept off toward the tram stop.

Andreas waited along with the rest of them, not participating in their whispered discussion. His silence was that of a man who doesn't want to give himself away, who is afraid that a careless remark might betray his closely guarded secret.

The man pulled back the curtain and called out the name, Andreas Pum, into the room. A few times Andreas Pum's crutches tapped on the ground, echoing in the renewed silence.

Suddenly, Andreas began to shake. He saw the head of the commission, a senior officer with a gold collar and a blond beard. Beard, face, and uniform collar blended into an impression of white and gold. 'Another shell-shock case,' somebody said. The crutches in Andreas's hands began to skitter across the floor all by themselves. A couple of orderlies leaped to their feet to assist him.

'License!' barked the voice of the senior officer. The orderlies sat Andreas down on a chair and got to work. They bent over their rustling papers with dancing pens.

Then Andreas hobbled out the door, with a sheaf of papers in his quivering hand.

When he came to pack his belongings, the trembling left him. He merely thought: A miracle has taken place! A miracle has taken place!

He stayed behind in the lavatory until all his comrades had gone. Then he counted up his money.

On the tram, people offered him their seats. He chose the best one, opposite the entrance, with his crutches lying beside him, right across the middle of the carriage, like a frontier post. Everyone was staring at Andreas.

He went to a shelter that he knew.

Chapter 3

THE BARREL ORGAN is manufactured by the firm of Dreccoli & Co. It has a box shape, and comes on a wooden stand that is collapsible and portable. Andreas carries his barrel organ on his back with a couple of straps, like a kit bag. The left side of the instrument has on it no fewer than eight screws. They are for the selection of the melody. The barrel organ has eight cylinders, among them the National Anthem and the 'Lorelei.'

Andreas Pum keeps his permit in his wallet, which used to be the leather cover of a notebook that he salvaged from a rubbish heap that he walks past every day. With his permit in his pocket, a man may walk serenely through the streets of the world, though they be swarming with policemen. One need fear no danger; indeed, there is none to fear. No denunciation from any ill-disposed, peevish neighbor need concern us. We write the authorities a postcard and tell them what it's about. We keep our remarks brief and to the point. Our permit puts us on a similar footing to the authorities. The government allows us to play wherever and whenever we please. We may set up our barrel organs on busy corners. Of course, within five minutes the police are there. Let them come! Surrounded by a ring of anxious onlookers, we pull out our permit. The police salute. We go on playing whatever we feel like: 'Don't

Cry, Little Girl,' 'The Girl with the Dark Eyes,' and 'The Boy Sat by the Fountain.' For a fashion-conscious audience we even have a waltz from last year's hit operetta.

Depending on his mood, Andreas can crank the handle so fast that the waltz comes out as brisk and martial as a march. Because naturally he sometimes has a hankering for a march, especially on cool, dull days when the pain in his amputated joint tells him there's rain on the way. His long-buried leg hurts him. The knee where it was taken off goes blue. The padding on the wooden peg isn't soft enough. The horsehair has already been worn away. Down or fur would have been more comfortable. On such days, Andreas has to wad the joint with a handkerchief or two. They aren't really enough.

As soon as it started raining, the pain disappeared. But there wasn't much money to be made on rainy days. The oilcloth, once gleaming, hard, and waterproof, was cracked in a few places; a kind of crazed map covered it now. If the rain got through the cover into the good wood beneath and then into the workings of the instrument, the cylinders would be ruined. Thank God it hadn't happened yet.

When it rained, Andreas would stand for hours in one of those kindly entryways where 'Begging and Hawking' were not explicitly forbidden, where no dog stood guard and no sullen porter or worse, porter's wife, protected the sanctity of the doorway. For Andreas had had a bellyful of abuse from the fair sex. Not that that prevented him from dreaming of the cruel tenderness of some still unspecified female hand that he might one day call his own.

Andreas's tastes were not conventional; the more vehement the oaths of the woman putting him to flight, the more grating the sound of her voice, the more menacing her figure, the better he liked it. Even as he turned to flee the inhospitable doorkeeper, he was as much thrilled by her womanliness as he was disappointed by the loss of potential earnings. Andreas had many such encounters. They were his only experiences. They would preoccupy his nights, filling his dreams with doughty women, and supplying the graver melodies of his hurdy-gurdy with a poetic text. Things reached such a pass that his instrument ceased to be mechanical to him, and he came to see virtuosity in his playing. For the yearnings, the apprehensiveness, and the sorrows of his spirit fed the hand that cranked the handle, and he thought he had the ability to play louder and softer, more feelingly or more militantly, according to his mood and his feelings. He came to love his instrument, and held a dialogue with it that only he could understand. Andreas Pum was a true musician.

When he wanted distraction, he would look at the colorful painting on the back panel of his hurdy-gurdy. It depicted the stage of a puppet theater and a part of the audience. Fair- and dark-haired children were gazing at the stage, on which exciting things were being enacted. A wild-looking gray-haired witch was holding a magic wand. In front of her stood two children with antlers sprouting from their heads. A doe was grazing above them. There was no doubt that the picture showed humans being transformed by an evil woman. Andreas had never considered the possibility of such things actually happening. But spending so much time poring over the picture as he did, it became as familiar to him and as believable as any other thing he might see on a daily basis. There was almost nothing fantastic left about such a transformation. Much more outlandish than the subject itself were the colors. Andreas's eyes drank in the rich glossy tones, and his soul grew intoxicated by the luscious harmony of a carmine red dissolving into the yearning orange of the evening sky.

He had plenty of time for such distraction at home. Home, admittedly, was not the sort of place where a man might spend an entire day. Rather, it meant a bed in what seemed to Andreas to be quite a spacious room. Apart from himself, a girl and her boyfriend stayed there. Her name was Klara, and his was Willi. She was the stand-in cashier in a small café, and he was an unemployed metalworker. Willi worked just one day a week, and not in his proper craft either. He pushed a handcart through the streets, buying up old newspapers. At the end of the day, he brought them to a scrap merchant. The man left him a third of what he brought in, seeing as he'd had to advance him the tiny start-up capital. It was evident that Willi couldn't live off his earnings. He was living off Klara. She had some earnings on the side. He was the jealous type. But at night, when they were both lying under the skimpy coverlet, he tried to forget what he was living off, and he succeeded too. In the morning he stayed in bed long after Klara and Andreas had left. He stayed at home all day, and refused to allow Andreas into the room until nightfall. He would justify this by saying: 'There's a time and a place for everything!' It wasn't that he took against the cripple, Andreas – not at all. He merely liked order. And so Andreas Pum had a billet, but nowhere to live. The way of the world is such that a man may only enjoy that for which he has paid.

Andreas was happy to abide by this dispensation too, and he would arrive shortly after dark. He made tea on a spirit burner. Willi drank the alcohol from it in a water glass. Andreas drank his tea, and ate a piece of bread with it. Sometimes Willi would supply a slice of sausage to go with it. Because it so happened that when Willi took a walk on a fine day, his route would take him past a delicatessen where the plump sausages hung in the doorway like hanged men. Then, more out of derring-do than for the sake of any larceny, Willi would cut down two or three of the sausages. It was the danger and the proof of his own skill that seduced him. Besides, it might have been accounted a sin if he had refused the offer of Fate. Andreas had his own idea of where the sausages might have come from. Once he asked Willi. 'Eat up and shut up,' said Willi, 'there's a time and a place for everything.'

Happily, it was no infraction of Willi's regulations if, while digesting his supper, Andreas gave himself over to a contemplation of the painting on his hurdy-gurdy. The incomplete transformation on the painting seemed to cry out to be taken further, and Andreas would have loved to do it himself. He would have transformed the two children still in human shape into does or some other creatures. There were so many possibilities. Couldn't children just as well be turned into rats? Eek! Rats! Or cats, or lion cubs, cute little crocodiles, lizards, bees, bird twitter! Actual birds. A good painter, someone who could handle brushes and paints, could easily paint a sequel.

Klara came in a little after midnight. She got undressed. Andreas peered at her through his half-shut eyelids, and got a sight of her in her chemise. He hoped for a glimpse of bare breast, and his heart thumped as he prayed for one of her shoulder straps to slip. Then he heard the sounds of kissing and embracing, and he fell asleep, dreaming of stout, broad-hipped widows, with a well-stacked shelf of bosom.

Ah, how he longed for a woman and a room and a double bed full of teeming warmth. Because the summer was now almost over, and he could guess at the horrors of winter. Andreas was all alone in the world. He had spent the previous winter in the hospital. Now the wintry streets were in prospect and sometimes they loomed in his face as steep and sheer as a sleigh run.

The street is our enemy. It really is as it appears to us, sheer and uphill. We only don't notice it when we stride along it. In winter, though – so the newspapers tell us – the porters and shop attendants, the ones who chase us out of buildings and courtyards, and throw hard words after us, forget to strew ashes or sand on the ice, and we fall, robbed of our mobility by the cold.

Andreas would have liked to get himself a woman before the winter, one of those tough, doughty, indomitable concierges who regularly put him to flight, and whose imposing stance was nevertheless etched in his mind's eye: he could see the fists jammed into the hips, making them bulge out still more, and the ass, taut, bulging, and white under the petticoats. To have such a woman to call his own – what strength, courage, and security that must give a man: a winter then would be child's play.

He was woken early by the effing and blinding of Willi, who had had his lie-in disturbed by Klara's getting up. Andreas went out onto the morning streets, and hobbled off hurriedly, with the hurrying crowds, as though impelled, not by the vague necessity of playing in some courtyard or other, but by the notion of having to reach one in particular, a very long way away. He had divided the city up into different districts, following his own personal method, and each day he would go to a different district. That way he could be sure of extending his knowledge of the city all the time, keen-eyed and curious, hobbling fearlessly along the smooth asphalt of wide avenues, cautiously bringing approaching automobiles to a stop with his lofted stick, and swearing at inconsiderate motorists. And so he learned to conquer the street, the dangerous street, which is the enemy of us all. He wasn't going to allow it to get him down, not at all. He had his permit.

A permit from the government, allowing him to play wher-ever and whenever he pleased. He had his crutches and his permit and his medal. Anyone could see he was an invalid, a soldier who had given his blood on behalf of the Fatherland. And at least there was still some respect for men like that. Woe betide anyone who failed to respect him!

Was he not fulfilling his duty when he played his hurdy-gurdy? Was not the permit pressed into his hands by the government in person, so to speak, as much an obligation as a concession? When he played, he relieved them of concern for his welfare, and relieved the country of a burdensome impost. Yes, there was no question that his occupation could only be compared with that of service to the state and his role with that of an official; especially when he selected from among his cylinders the National Anthem.

Chapter 4

IT WAS IN THE PESTALOZZISTRASSE, on a warm Thursday, and specifically in the courtyard of No. 37 (opposite the yellow brick church, which had assembled a green lawn around itself, in the middle of the road, as though to emphasize its distinctness from all the other houses), that Andreas Pum was overwhelmed by the desire to play a march, possibly because both his own increasing torpor and that of the day made some sort of rousing interruption essential.

Andreas set the screw on the left of the hurdy-gurdy to 'National Anthem' and cranked the handle so violently that the stately sounds lost their solemnity and began skipping and leaping, forgot their pauses, and actually did have some remote resemblance to a march tune.

Five children were standing in the courtyard, and two housemaids leaned raptly out of their windows. A woman dressed in black emerged from the passage behind Andreas, strode purposefully, almost mannishly, up to him, and stopped. She laid a heavy hand on Andreas Pum's shoulder, and said: 'My Gustav passed away yesterday. Will you play something melancholy for him?'

Though no shrinking violet, Andreas was nevertheless taken aback, and he removed his hand from the crank in the vertical position and turned to look. He was sorry that, as he did, the warm and powerful hand slipped hesitantly but unavoidably from his shoulder. He looked into the widow's puffy face. It appealed to him. He didn't have time to estimate her age, but he instantly appreciated that this blond woman dressed in black was a widow in what were commonly called 'the best years.' At this stage, Andreas didn't take his appreciation any further. At the most, a dim sense spread through him that this woman had entered his life at the same time as she had entered the courtyard. He felt as though a light were beginning to dawn in his soul.

'With pleasure,' said Andreas, and inclined his head. As though a melancholy tune required special preparation, he self-importantly unscrewed the cylinder with the National Anthem, turned the crank down to the bottom, causing the last trapped note to escape the box like a half-stifled yawn. Thereupon, Andreas turned the fourth-last screw. For a second, he had hesitated between 'Lorelei' and 'The Boy Sat by the Fountain.' He plumped for the 'Lorelei,' assuming the widow would be more familiar with it.

This proved to be the case. The widow, having retired to her room to enjoy the melancholy tune in comfort at her window, began to sing. She anticipated the sounds of the instrument, as though driven by impatience and a desire to prove to herself and anyone listening that she knew the tune by heart, and was not dependent on any barrel organ; meanwhile Andreas, unfazed by the woman's haste, thought a particularly slow rendition was called for, and he executed slow turns of the handle, to allow the full melancholy of the tune to unfold. Also, he felt himself in the sort of ceremonial mood that overcomes us at decisive turns of our lives and that we like to mark with an uncommon gravitas.

After he had spun out the 'Lorelei' for a full quarter of

an hour, the widow came down into the courtyard, carrying cake and bread and a bag of fruit. Andreas thanked her. The widow said: 'My name is Blumich, my maiden name was Menz. Come and see me again after the funeral.' Andreas felt it appropriate to take her hand. He did so, squeezing her closed fist in his fingers, saying: 'My condolences, Frau Blumich.'

That day he played no more. He betook himself to a bench in front of the church, ate up the cake and the fruit, and stowed the bread in his knapsack. He got home later than usual. Willi had long since surrendered to the imperative to stretch out on his bed, and was only putting off the moment of losing consciousness, for fear that he would be woken up later, and have to get out of bed to let 'the cripple' in. When Andreas walked in, Willi didn't respond to his greeting. Andreas felt hurt. This was a day when he felt particularly well disposed toward Willi. He got out the spirit burner to make his tea. Willi was nettled by his silence. He was longing to have an argument with Andreas. And so he said: 'If you're this late again tomorrow, I'll smash up your hurdy-gurdy. I insist on punctuality! There's a time and a place for everything!' But it was even harder to provoke Andreas today than usual. He smiled at Willi, put his bread on the table, and said politely, with the gallantry of a man of the world: 'Help yourself, Mr. Willi.'

'I want you back punctually!' said Willi, joining him at the table. He's a good guy, really! he thought, and already felt reconciled. He had a sausage left from his latest sortie. It was hanging on a nail over the bed. Gently he looped it off, broke it in two, and gave half to Andreas.

'I met a woman today,' confessed Andreas.

'Congratulations!' said Willi.

'She's a widow by the name of Blumich.'

'Young?'

'Yes, young.'

'Lucky beggar!'

'Her husband died yesterday.'

'And she's already—?'

'No!'

'I would get a move on, pal! Widows don't wait around!'

Andreas remembered that piece of advice. He didn't think of Willi as an outstanding specimen of humanity, but he had to admit that people of his type were more knowledgeable about women, and had garnered plenty of experience. Perhaps it might be an idea to attend the funeral? But maybe that was unseemly because of the neighbors – and it would displease Frau Blumich? It almost pained him that he didn't know her first name. In his innermost thoughts, he kept having to refer to her as 'Frau Blumich,' though he felt she wasn't a stranger to him anymore. The more he thought about her, the closer he felt to her. There was no one in the world who meant more to him. Although he couldn't prove it, he thought there was no one he meant more to either. For wasn't it the loss of a husband to which he, Andreas, owed her acquaintance and her kindness to him? Did a woman forget so easily? And if she could was she still worth knowing? Who really knew the first thing about women? Who could say how long her husband might have been ill, a living corpse? How long the poor thing might have had to constrain her naturally joyous nature? Andreas was shaken with sympathy for her.

Today again he left his eyelids open a crack, and he tried to catch a glimpse of the girl's bosom. But it wasn't envy that moved him, but the wish to compare. Those brief moments in the courtyard had been enough to give him a sense of Frau

Blumich's person. Ah, she was stout, and he could see how the skimpy dress had had to fight to contain the thrusting assertive bosom; how her broad hips pressed powerfully and desirously against her girdle; how it was all healthy plenitude, and nowhere excessive. Life and pleasure flowed from her warm hands, and her brown, slightly tear-reddened eyes were like two bold beacons of desire.

Now, was a man like Andreas worthy of such a woman? What did he have to offer her? He was healthy, though his missing leg sometimes hurt him when there was rain in prospect. But that was really to do with poor living. He was strong, broad-shouldered, with an imposingly thin, bony nose, bulging muscles, thick brown hair, and – when he made an effort and tensed his expression – the keen, eagle look of a warrior, especially when his dark, not remotely grizzled mustache was teased out on both sides and greased with pomade. Nor was he a green youth in matters of love, and now, after a long period of chastity, he was full of strength and manliness. He was indeed just the man to satisfy a fastidious widow.

With these proud thoughts, Andreas fell asleep, and with them he woke up. For the first time in ages, he looked long and exactingly in the mirror, as he had before the roll call in his army days. He breathed on his metal cross and polished it on his sleeve until it shone. He had to recomb his hair three times, before he found the correct parting. Then he made straight for the Pestalozzistrasse.

On his way, it occurred to him that he didn't shave often enough. He went twice a week, on Tuesdays and Fridays, to the barbers' apprentice school, where the young apprentices scraped chins, painfully but for free. That apprentice school and the twice-weekly interval both now struck Andreas as unworthy of a man who intended to make a profound and lasting impression on a spruce widow. And that reckless exaltation that so blissfully defeats us when we are certain of making a conquest now gripped Andreas Pum and quite overpowered his generally alert and thoughtful character. Andreas went into a barbershop that gloried, not for nothing, in the name of salon, and there he encountered – in spite of the bemusement that his hurdy-gurdy provoked – the same cordial warmth and politeness that, like a mild spring breeze, wafts out democratically to greet anyone entering a barbershop.

He beheld himself in the mirror, his face white with powder, his parting glistening with ointment, and with pride and satisfaction he breathed in the spicy aroma he gave off. He resolved henceforth no longer to patronize the apprentice school but instead to seek out various legitimate establishments more frequently. He flexed his scalp and his forehead, and produced the two impressive little wrinkles either side of his nose, thereby creating the aquiline expression that he had always put on at decisive points in his military career. Then he slipped on his hurdy-gurdy with such a lofty movement that he almost resembled a sergeant in the accounting corps, buckling on his sword.

Reservations of various kinds and degrees of importance assailed him on the street in front of No. 37, like an annoying swarm of flies. He struck himself as a flint-hearted egoist, a cold and vain man, who, without any regard to Frau Blumich's day – perhaps the saddest of her life – had gone out and dandified himself for her. What would she make of him when he appeared in front of her like that, having seen him only the day before in his customary state? Would she not quite justifiably feel offended, stricken, even hurt? Perhaps it wasn't a good idea at all to visit the widow Blumich today. He ought to feel a little regard for her dead husband, too, who wasn't even in the ground. There were really plenty of reasons for Andreas to be patient, to give the widow time to come to terms with her loss. Last but not least, she herself had asked him – summoned him – not for today, but for tomorrow.

On that day, Andreas Pum enjoyed more good fortune than at any time since he had begun wandering through courtyards with his hurdy-gurdy. Perhaps it was because the unseasonable heat forced everyone to keep their windows wide open, and the music afforded them the perfect pretext to lean out of their windows and have a breather, or because the clean-shaven, tidy Andreas, decorated with his gleaming cross, struck them as being particularly deserving – we don't know the reason, but the coins rained down on Andreas so plentifully that he got tired of bending down to pick them up. There was no doubt about it: his fortunes had changed with the entrance of the widow Blumich into his life. And, smiling sweetly and gently, to match the rays of the setting sun on the gables of the houses, Andreas set off for home, long before it began to get dark, with a warm greeting for Willi on his lips and the healthy appetite that so often accompanies a sense of satisfaction.

Chapter 5

AS YET, ANDREAS WAS unaware of his rival, who, in view of his occupation, might very well be termed a dangerous one. This was a fellow resident of No. 37, the youthful, slender, and consummately seductive deputy police inspector, Vinzenz Topp. A local Romeo wherever his duty took him, a man able to combine official dignity with a personable warmth, he was cordial to passersby and junior colleagues and possessed an admirable correctness, blended with soldierly humility in the presence of superior officers. That blending itself had a personal note, so that not only did Vinzenz seem better turned out than his comrades but more himself as well. He was personable on duty, and professional in his daily life.

During her husband's long illness, Frau Blumich, her senses sharpened by abstinence, had become aware of her neighbor's good points in all their dazzling profusion, not infrequently exchanging smiling greetings with him. She was quite clear in her own mind, though, that, while the Deputy Inspector might well serve as a brief distraction for women in sorry straits, he was not dependable husband material. Moreover, he had night duty three times a week. Frau Blumich was afraid, all alone with her little five-year-old in her two small rooms that felt cavernous at night, in the dark. And while, in a general way, she had confidence in her ability to tame and rein in such men as didn't mind a bit of variety, she did think the youthful exuberance of a Vinzenz Topp might be too much for her. Unfortunately, neither were her instincts sufficiently infallible, nor her mind sufficiently sharp for her to realize how much the Deputy Inspector in fact thirsted for the stability of married life at the side of a widow. Because, basically, Vinzenz Topp was dissatisfied with his existence. He was gradually slipping into the period of life in which it was becoming irksome to expend time and attention, not to mention money, on the ever-changing objects of his affections. The heart yearns eventually for the regulated calm of a lawful wedded life. We weary of forever traveling hopefully, so to speak, to still our natural desire for the warmth and proximity of a female form. Our profession already makes us homeless. We need a home, sweet home, from which occasional forays are not to be excluded, silently to be forgiven us. We require our own – under present circumstances quite unattainable – two-bedroom apartment, furnished, and a generous family supplement in view of our changed circumstances. And finally we desire our promotion to the rank of inspector, not that that depends on matrimony, but it may be accelerated by a hint as to our increased needs to a superior favorably inclined.

Of all of this, as we have said, Frau Blumich – given name Katharina – had no inkling. She was used to making an impression on men, and she found nothing remarkable about the fact that Vinzenz Topp now also had sent in her direction some of those appraising-cum-respectful glances that all women know to appreciate. She collected glances like that on a daily basis, in the building, on the street, in the park, and in the shops. They didn't signify anything. Men are constitutionally averse to shouldering responsibility; they don't want to make their beds, but they certainly want to lie in them. Katharina Blumich had her feet firmly on the ground. She had selected her first husband carefully as well. The fact that he got TB from working in the brush factory was an act of God. There was nothing to be done about fate, but that was no reason to go and lose your head. And reason argued for a man of a certain age, possibly with some physical handicap, though not one that would get in the way of marital happiness; reason counseled a bird whose wings had already been clipped, because that would be easier to keep and required less in the way of strenuous training. His class was actually fairly immaterial, seeing as Frau Blumich thought it more practical to raise a creature from some lower sphere into her own, rather than suffer herself to be pulled aloft. That would have enjoined her to be grateful, and her authority would have been eroded as a consequence. And of course the paramount thing in a household is the authority of the woman running it.

And so Frau Katharina Blumich decided she would forgo Deputy Inspector Vinzenz Topp. He could make someone else unhappy if he wanted. Let him go and spend his life around loose women. As a constant threat to any eventual husband and a potential object of jealousy, he was always handily available anyway. Everything must be put to use, but one mustn't throw oneself away.

The day Andreas Pum paid his first official visit to the courtyard of No. 37 was dull and overcast, an anticipation of autumn in spite of its late-summer sultriness, the air full of moisture that hurt Andreas in his missing leg. On such days he felt like a child anyway, abandoned, yearning, melancholy, in need of protection. No sooner had he launched into the 'Lorelei,' the tacitly agreed signal between them, than Frau

Blumich appeared, and asked him to adjourn to her apartment and play for her there. It was a sad, mournful melody that did nothing to diminish his sadness.

After the music there was a polite curtsy from pallid little Anni, who had her thin plait in a black, batlike bow that was much too big for her. After the recent sad disturbances, the child was silent and bewildered. She took to the man with the wooden leg and the musical instrument right away. She became quite trusting. She was five, an age when one is still an understanding god, able to see the hidden kindness of other people like brightly colored pebbles in a clear mountain stream.

The conversation flowed, punctuated by coffee and home-made cake, a kind of quiet wake for the late Herr Blumich. 'He had a wonderful wardrobe,' enthused the woman, 'and he was just about your size, too. A couple of brown suits that are barely five years old. He was still a soldier at the time; how I worried about him, now I wish he'd died then, maybe the loss would have been easier to bear, and the girl wouldn't have been either, poor orphaned thing! Oh, you've no idea what it is to be a woman all alone in this wicked world. How could you know, how could a man know that.'

'My mother, God rest her, was widowed in her young years as well,' Andreas volunteered.

'And did she remarry?'

'Yes, a plumber.'

'Was he good to her?'

'Yes, very good.'

'Is he alive still?'

'No, both of them died during the War.'

'Both in the War?'

'Yes, both of them.'

'Well, if you're lucky enough, and your second husband turns out to be a good and faithful helpmate as well . . .' At this point, Frau Blumich thought a little crying was called for. She looked for her handkerchief, found it, and began.

Andreas, quite rightly, thought this sad scene was a fortunate turn of events for himself. Now he might chance his arm. And bending over the sobbing woman, brushing against her breast almost inadvertently, he said:

'I will always be true to you.'

Frau Blumich removed her handkerchief and asked, almost sharply: 'Really?'

'As I'm sitting here now.'

Frau Blumich stood up and kissed Andreas on the forehead. He reached for her mouth. She fell onto his lap. She stayed sitting there.

'Where are you living now?' she asked.

'In a pension,' replied Andreas.

'It's just because of people talking. Otherwise you could move in tomorrow. I think we should wait for four weeks.'

'As long as that?' asked Andreas, and threw both his arms around Katharina, feeling the stately softness of her body and repeating plaintively: 'As long as that?'

Katharina broke away with a determined movement. 'What must be must be,' she said sternly and so convincingly that Andreas quickly came around to her way of thinking, even as he began daydreaming of their delicious future.

Chapter 6

WHAT A LUCKY FELLOW he was! This sort of thing didn't happen every day, it wasn't a common occurrence, it was a miracle. How many people there were in his position, trembling at the prospect of the winter, like frail plants, knowing they are abandoned and condemned to death, and without even the strength to cut short the slow creep of fate with a swift suicide. But now he, Andreas Pum, had been selected from among thousands of invalids, by the widow Katharina Blumich, whom already he had taken to thinking of as 'Kathi.' His now was the warm, big-bosomed, round-hipped woman of his dreams; a broody softness emanated from her body, a yearning and narcotic scent, the almost-forgotten scent of a woman, that seems to swell as the flesh swells, like a bosom, a billowing, pillowing scent.

Katharina Blumich had many good points. At certain moments, Andreas thought of himself as having almost as many. He was a man of rare gifts of spirit. Devout, mild, law-abiding, and dwelling in complete harmony with divine and human laws. A man as beloved of the priesthood as he was of officialdom, respected, nay, decorated by the government, with no criminal record, a brave soldier, no revolutionary, implacably opposed to heathens, drunkards, thieves, and housebreakers. What a difference between him and, say, Willi. Between him and all those others, those hordes who played and sang in courtyards without any authorization! Terrified at the echoing footfall of policemen, always vulnerable to denunciation from a malicious neighbor, frittering away their meager earnings at the bar, pimps and crooks that they were! How many such specimens Andreas could have produced from his hospital time alone, where the wards were acrawl with godless individuals! How many had ugly, disfiguring, and highly infectious diseases! He felt sorry for the women! They didn't know what they were letting themselves in for! Whereas Andreas was pure in body and spirit, he had gone through life as though inoculated against sins and sufferings, an obedient son to his father, and later on a briskly compliant subordinate to his superiors. He didn't covet the goods of the wealthy. He didn't go clambering through the windows of their villas. He had never mugged anyone in the shady alleys of the parks. And now Fate was rewarding him for all that by giving him an exemplary woman to be his wife. Everyone makes his own luck, really. He deserved his. Nothing will come of nothing. Only rebels think differently. And they're mistaken. They never learn.

Suddenly something darkened Andreas's cheery flow of thought. He remembered Bossi, the blacksmith, and his own trembling in front of the committee, which had got him his permit. What if that sort of thing were to happen again? Who could tell if the seed of shaking wasn't present in his limbs, in his body, in his bloodstream, if it wouldn't burst into flower again at the wrong moment, to overpower and destroy poor Andreas? How had it come about that among all those men he had been the one to be singled out for a permit, and without being condemned to lifelong shaking? Would Fate not perhaps one day ask for its debt to be discharged? He wanted to be sure, to consult a doctor.

A doctor? We are rightly suspicious of doctors. We sicken in their waiting rooms. While they look for our affliction with their hands, their instruments, their knowledge, it will attack us, something we never suffered from before. The doctor's spectacles, his white gown, its smell, the deadly cleanliness of his jars and pincers condemn us to death. For there is a God, higher than all doctors, who determines the state of our health; and since He has been so good to us thus far, He positively encourages us to put our trust in Him.

Andreas's nights were always swarming with these thoughts and fears, now horrid, now kindly. Oh, it was probably just his yearning for Katharina Blumich. The days, though, that are full of the bustle of others and our own activity, the bright streets and the rushing crowds, the children in the courtyards and the housemaids at the windows, the days – though they have nothing in common with our heart's desire – give us the comforting assurance that we will attain it. Most of all, each day concluded with an afternoon in the house of Frau Blumich – Kathi – with coffee and whispered love talk. This consisted by no means of fatuous or sheepish professions of desire, fervent or stammered, but followed practical ends, and showed the great advantages of female wisdom, which is of such enduring appeal.

'We need to expand the business,' said Katharina. 'We should buy a little donkey and cart, so you don't have to go on lugging your hurdy-gurdy around with you.'

What luminous intelligence! What a dear inspiration: to purchase a donkey!

The donkey is a stupid but long-suffering animal, thought Andreas. He had often heard it said. A donkey has endurance. It was an animal tailor-made for our purposes. Moreover, it would be an asset to him in the streets and courtyards.

'What shall we call it?' Katharina asked.

No, really! She thought of everything. What could you call a donkey?

Rover was a dog's name.

'What about Mooli,' Katharina suggested. Mooli was a great idea.

Every day, before it got dark, Kathi would ask: 'Will you love Anni?'

To which, in all honesty, Andreas could not have given an answer. But he took little Anni, who was no longer so clean as she'd been on the first day, by the hand, and truly believed he felt a completely new, fatherly feeling for the girl. She was a quiet child, which made her seem thoughtful. Quiet children always seem to us like shrewd observers, and we find it flattering when they like us.

Without realizing it, Andreas took the lively warmth of the little girl's hand with him on his long and lonely walk home. Sometimes he would think of Anni with the joyful expectation that before long she, too, would become his very own. Hours later, he could still feel her soft little fist in the hollow of his hand like a little bird. How was it that you could forget other things you'd touched, but not Anni's fist? Maybe hands had their own memory! Stuff and nonsense! Their own memory! Odd thoughts you had when you were happy.

Two weeks had passed since Andreas had met his be-trothed. And he would probably have had to wait out another two for the beginning of their new life together, had nature not taken a hand in the proceedings.

One afternoon, while Kathi was making coffee, a storm blew up that rattled the open windows. It grew suddenly dark. Rain started to fall. Either Katharina had long hoped some unexpected natural phenomenon would assist her inclination to cut short the time she and her Andreas were waiting, or else the sudden violence of the storm had brought her to that conclusion. Whatever, Katharina abruptly and decisively said:

'You can spend the night here. I wouldn't put a dog out in this weather.'

The following morning Andreas moved in. He said goodbye to Willi and sent his regards to Klara. Willi carried his suitcase to the tram stop, whistling a jaunty provocative little tune. He buried both his hands in his pockets and strode complacently beside the hobbling Andreas. The small but heavy wooden suitcase he carried on a strap over his shoulder, as though it were a shopping bag or an empty basket. This demonstration of Willi's strength amounted to a tacit acknowledgment of Andreas's departure. And the cheery tune he was whistling voiced the pang of separation. At the tram stop he muttered 'All the best then, pal!' through gritted teeth – and he turned and sauntered off back home, throwing a long look down the side street to the delicatessen that had the sausages dangling outside the door, solid and chubby like fat corpses.

IT WAS UNAVOIDABLE that, within a few days, Andreas would make the acquaintance of the Deputy Inspector of Police and receive his congratulations. The meeting took place in the presence of Frau Katharina, who failed to observe the pain that Vinzenz Topp was hiding behind his suave manner. To have a cripple preferred to himself, the best-knit man in the area, to have his rank, his uniform, and his knowledge all set at naught, to have his experience of the fair sex rendered unavailing, and his innuendo futile – all that deeply pained Vinzenz Topp. He resolved not to like this new husband of Katharina Blumich's, a mistake on the part of this otherwise clever woman. He barely nodded when he and Andreas met on the stairs.

But Andreas noticed nothing, because he was living in a new and numbing blissfulness, which armors us against the offenses and hurts of the world, and, like a kindly veil, obscures the wickedness of mankind.

Yes, Andreas was happy. A goddess warmed his bed, and turned it into a paradise. No pain reminded him of his missing leg. In its freshly padded extension, his stump was as warmly cushioned as if it were in the hollow of a woman's loving hand. Mornings were ushered in with a steaming cup of coffee. The day ended with a hot meal. His pockets were full of sandwiches, accompanying him on his way like the affectionate thoughts of his wife. In the evening hours, pale, staring-eyed Anni perched on his good knee, while Andreas explained to her the wonderful meaning of the picture on his hurdy-gurdy.

'What a sweet little thing you are,' he would often say, because he wasn't able to come up with anything more original to say about Anni.

Slowly, with a great, beneficent, healing warmth, love blossomed in him.

They were married early in November. For the last time that autumn, the sun shone so warmly that people stood around in shirtsleeves like in spring outside the church (which was of yellow brick, surrounded by a quietly frost-covered lawn), and little Anni didn't get cold without a coat, in her thin white muslin dress. She looked like a miniature bride herself.

Then came days of gray rain and cold. Andreas restricts his playing to the mornings. He isn't cold. The persistent rain fails to soak him. He doesn't miss the sun, hiding behind the clouds. Thanks to his new wooden leg with its sharp edges, he never misses his footing on the slippery pavement. He walks along the edge of the pavement, with Mooli, the little donkey, ahead of him, pulling the handcart with his hurdy-gurdy. All of it is Andreas's property. He has begun to think of investing in a parrot with red and green feathers for the springtime. Children and grown-ups stop to look and listen. In spite of the cold, money continues to rain down from all the windows in all the courtyards. In spite of the cold, passersby reach into their inside pockets for him. Everyone knows him – no, not everyone, but a lot of people all the same. What does he lack, Andreas Pum?

He loves everything in the world, and most of all two – are they things or people? They belong together, though they're of different species. Andreas loves Anni and he loves Mooli, he loves the little girl and the donkey.

He has built a little shelter for the donkey in the courtyard. At night, it sometimes occurs to him that Mooli might be cold. He thinks of laying in more straw in the morning.

There are posters on the hoardings. The war invalids are playing up again. Typical heathen behavior! 'Comrades!' the posters shriek. The government! The government! They want to bring down the government! He, Andreas Pum, wasn't going to fall for that nonsense. He didn't go around creating a disturbance, he was a quiet man, he detested drunkards and rebels and card players.

With his heart thus full of scorn, Andreas Pum might have lived out the greater or lesser number of years allotted to him by Fate, with his heart full of scorn, in that good, warm contentment, in that perfect harmony with the laws of heaven and earth, as beloved of priests as by the officials of the government – had not a complete stranger entered Andreas Pum's life and destroyed it, not out of malice, but compelled by a blind Fate to be a hapless tool in the hand of the devil, who on occasion, all unbeknown to us, comes between ourselves and the Almighty; so that we are still sending our prayers up to Him in the comforting certainty that He is there, watching over us – and are astonished not to be heard by Him. The cause of Andreas's misfortune was one Herr Arnold, a director of the haberdashery firm of Arnold & Hahn.

Chapter 7

HERR ARNOLD WAS BIG, healthy, well fed, and dissatisfied. His business was thriving. At home he had a faithful spouse who had borne him two children: a boy and a girl, just as he had wished. His suits fitted him, his ties were always fashionable, his wristwatch kept good time, his day was divided up with a pleasing precision. No disagreeable surprise was capable of disrupting his calm and well-regulated existence. It seemed almost unimaginable that the morning post could ever contain something like an irritating begging letter from an impoverished relative. He had no poor relatives. He came from a prosperous and well-ordered family. All its members shared a soothing freedom from care, and a similarity of outlook, of political views, of manifesting personal taste, of disdaining fashion, or participating in it. The Arnold home wasn't subject to those domestic calamities whose cause is usually to be found in a burned dinner. Even the children did well at school, behaved themselves, and seemed to understand their responsibility to the family name and its not inconsiderable traditions.

And yet Herr Arnold was afflicted by a chronic, and, as we see, wholly unreasonable dissatisfaction. He himself could think of some reasons, mind you. Contemporary politics upset him. He had inherited from his ancestors a pronounced love of order, and he felt certain contemporary tendencies were hell-bent on destroying the various forms of order. Furthermore, he was reaching that age when a paterfamilias requires a little erotic variety to restore his inner equilibrium. This yearning for love, in turn, created in him a measure of instability that threatened to wreck the order of his days and, still more, his nights, and that gradually spread throughout the whole range of Herr Arnold's activities, affecting his business dealings and even the conduct of his correspondence; this last most of all because Herr Arnold was in the habit of dictating letters to young Veronika Lenz* – who might have been given that name on purpose.

Now, Fräulein Lenz was as good as engaged. Even so, a man more practiced in matters of seduction would not have allowed himself to be deterred by such a circumstance. But it was precisely his want of experience that had thus far characterized Herr Arnold, emphasized his solidity, been the basis for his reputation, and given him the strength to wax indignant at the destructive manifestations of the society in which he lived. Oh, how he dreaded the day when he would come out in contradiction to his whole life, and how at the same time he yearned for that day to come! How careful he had to be at every hour, of himself, of his commercial partner, his wife, and his children. And how difficult he found it!

Because it was anything but easy to set aside Veronika Lenz, a blonde with capable hands and unexpectedly delicate features, dressed in a highly becoming way that gave the most important parts of her body an exciting prominence. She was unforgettable, especially on those days when she came to work in a dark green short-sleeved blouse that exposed

* A German poeticism for 'Spring' (Trans.)

the dark mole in the warm, shady crook of her elbow. It was there that Herr Arnold desired to place a kiss.

He did not doubt that, once he had put his mind to it, he would be successful. For his broad-shouldered, reddish-blond brand of manliness was bound to impress her; even if his face was spoiled by a hereditary defect that had shown up in various members of the Arnold clan over the centuries. Herr Arnold had a flat, crooked nose. It was caused by a crookedness of the septum, which meant that one of his nostrils was round, while the other was triangular. Still, Mother Nature, kindly even in her malice, endeavored to make up for this deficiency by making the tip of his nose fleshy, flat, and mobile. Its flexibility was such that it could sometimes make the disparity between his nostrils seem like a passing distortion, caused, as it might be, by his having blown his nose too vigorously. The casual observer was further deceived by a bushy red mustache, which drew attention to itself at the expense of its upper neighbor, and made the nose appear a feature of diminished importance.

All other aspects of the Arnold physique were of incontestable manliness. When he strode through the office, giving dictation, the floorboards groaned under his mighty sole. He was given to pausing on one foot, his hands in his jacket pockets, body leaning forward, only touching the carpet with the toe of his trailing foot, in the attitude of a statue that catches a man in mid-step. Two or three seconds like that, and only then would he take his next step. His strides were greatly long and ate up the ground. His dictation was harsh, and his epistolary style was chiding and menacing, even when the letters themselves were utterly formulaic. Even though Herr Arnold had been signing letters on behalf of the firm for more than a decade now, he still took pleasure in his signature. However many times he executed it, it was always a confirmation of the Arnoldian power, and – even as a graphic emblem – an imposing ornament. Therefore he liked to put his name to a document in a breathless hush, speedily and yet carefully, with the blotter in his left hand, all ready to absorb the shock of his ink-glistening name.

All the while, Veronika Lenz would stand behind his chair, bewitching her boss, without at all meaning to. It was certain that she had no other thought in mind than the diligent typing of the correspondence, and the punctual leaving of her workplace. But it was on this point that Herr Arnold had his doubts. For however little he understood about the lives of modern young women, he was convinced of one thing: that someone who was as good as engaged could not be classed as betrothed. That description alone would have filled him with that reverent shudder that we feel in the presence of sacred and holy names. Not even in our dreams may we contemplate sinful relationships with the betrothed of another. It would be almost tantamount to adultery. The theft of another's property. A cowardly theft. We live in a world where our neighbor's property is sacred. Imagine if it were not! On the other hand, an engagement that has not yet been announced, and that, under certain circumstances, might never be announced, is not the same as holy matrimony, no sir. Indeed, it's much more like some altogether less sacred relationship that doesn't command any particular respect – especially if one knows that the man in question is a good-for-nothing, a comic performer, an artiste, forever touring the cities of the world, probably with a girl waiting for him in each of them. It's not possible to rob a man like that. He doesn't lose anything. Quite the opposite – one might be accomplishing a divine purpose by opening the eyes of that girl, sharpening her scant sense of the bitter realities of life, which may only be forgotten and overcome in short, fleeting, and above all inconsequential ecstasies.

Once Herr Arnold had, by such careful reflections, succeeded in converting the exceptional state of his infatuation into an ordinary urge to do good in the world, he lost his fear of whatever difficulties stood in the way of his conquest. And so it came to pass that one day, while signing, he slowly set down his blotter, stood his pen in the inkwell, and – suddenly remembering that you can't leave a pen in ink without damaging it – immediately put it carefully back on its iron stand. Thereupon he turned his head, raised both his arms, and embraced the sweet bowed neck of the young blonde.

Veronika Lenz pushed up against the grasping hands, but their grip was stronger and prevailed. Thoroughly alarmed, and groaning in vain resistance, she felt her face approaching Herr Arnold's neck. She glimpsed the tufts of reddish hair that sprouted from his ears, smelled the odor of cigar smoke and human fat that escaped through the crack between the man's neck and his shirt-collar. The back of the chair cut into her painfully. She closed her eyes, as in the expectation of death, and then she felt a bite on her cheek.

Only then did she violently jerk her head back; she spat on Herr Arnold's neck, grabbed her jacket, hat, and bag, and stormed out.

Arnold had only one thing to hope for: that the girl, whom he now hated, would never come back. He decided to transfer a sizable sum of money to her immediately. He would get over this embarrassing incident in time. You got over all sorts of things. Work and don't despair! Chin up! Even the cleverest fellow is guilty of stupidity at some time. And already he was dreaming it was a year later, and the event was buried under the weight of 365 industrious and profitable days.

Thus calming his agitated soul, he drove home in his automobile, walked into his house with a loud, condescending greeting, kissed his still presentable wife on both cheeks, promised Christmas presents to the children, said something appropriate to the maid, and poured his bounty over the house. Then he slept deeply, healthily, and long, and in the morning he drove to work with a merry whistle on his lips.

There, Luigi Bernotat, a birdcall imitator from the Rococo Music Hall, destroyed Herr Arnold's newly found confidence. Luigi Bernotat, a man of exquisite manners, began by apologizing for calling on him so early and unannounced, and went on, unerringly, to speak of his betrothed, who, following a lamentable advance on the part of a certain gentleman, had seen herself forced to quit this otherwise reputable business and demand compensation.

'With pleasure,' Herr Arnold interrupted Luigi Bernotat's well-ordered exposition.

'That's all very well,' said Bernotat, 'but it's no more than your obligation. In addition, as the lady's intended, I feel I've been gravely offended. I have come therefore to let you know that I am taking you to court, that I am quite determined to take you to court – not least to make an example of you.'

A menacing pause ensued.

Herr Arnold picked up a shiny metal ruler, pressing his finger against the cool steel. It felt soothing, and at least a part of him gained temporary respite from the sudden sensation of burning that had come over him. Blackmail, that's his game, blackmail, and I've laid myself open to it, laid myself open to it, Herr Arnold thought to himself. Then he stood up and said: 'How much do you want?'

Luigi Bernotat seemed to have been waiting for the question. Like an actor hearing his cue, he embarked slowly and confidently on a speech, with pauses for effect and occasional very rapid passages for contrast, and his voice so compelled its listener that after a short time he was only listening to the rising and falling tone, without thinking of interrupting.

'I suppose,' said Luigi Bernotat, 'you take me for a blackmailer? Ach, what else could you think? People of your sort are bound to believe that every man's honor has its price. Well, mine doesn't! Not mine, Herr Arnold. You yourself will admit the rashness of what you attempted. There are still courts, thankfully. You never imagined an artist would be so persnickety. You'd never have laid a finger on the betrothed of a business associate of yours, or a lawyer's, or a student's or an officer's. I mean to teach you that an artist's fiancée is not there for the taking either. I might have challenged you to a duel, but for the fact that I belong to an anti-dueling society. And don't make the mistake of supposing I'm a coward. I have a reputation. You will have heard of Martin Popovics, the wind artist. I slapped his face twice for a stupid joke he made. I'm an amateur boxer. As you see, I'm not a coward. But I won't betray my principles either. The most important thing in life is to be true to oneself. Now you be true to yourself, and take the consequences!'

Herr Arnold stood there silently, incapable of speech. He stared at his opponent's red, black, and brown striped tie, which pertly stuck out past the ends of his collar, like a perquisite for joie de vivre. It felt very quiet after Luigi Bernotat had delivered his peroration. Then all at once, Bernotat began to trill. He was showing his cheeky exuberance by doing a perfect rendition of a lark. His whistling grew louder and louder, until it was like a whole larks' chorus.

Herr Arnold yelled: 'Don't you whistle at me, you cheeky pup.'

Luigi Bernotat bowed. 'That's for you to prove,' he said quietly, and, in a rather different style, after another bow, he sashayed quietly out.

In spite of his agitation, Herr Arnold was under no illusion about the very grave import of the visit. What had he done! Forty-five years of an irreproachable life, a stainless reputation, a glittering business career, all were under threat. Barely pausing to reflect further, he drove to his lawyer.

Of course he was away in court. Stupid of him to expect anything else! What do we have lawyers for anyway? So they can disappear the minute we want their advice. Our personal physicians? So they can come and write out our death certificates, once we're dead. Our secretaries? So they can plunge us into crisis over a silly joke. Our wives? Not even possible to talk to them, when our hearts are full; our misfortune only serves to appease their eternal lust for vengeance. Our children? They've got their own lives to lead, and we, their fathers, are only obstacles at best.

All this might have been the case for hundreds of years. Yet many of the features of this particular case of Bernotat, Lenz, and Arnold could be blamed on this modern epoch, these shocking times, which were so hell-bent on destroying the various forms of order. In what other period of history would it have been conceivable for a little office girl to send her fiancé along to see her employer? For her 'betrothed' – Herr Arnold could only think of him in ironic quotation marks – to go to the head of a venerable business, and demand of him that he answer for his conduct – a betrothed, at that, who was something in a circus! In what other period of history would the yeasty froth of society have mustered so much barefaced impertinence?

Herr Arnold sent his car away, and walked around for a while. He ate his dinner in a restaurant. So what if his family were worried about him. Where did it say he was obliged to go home punctually night after night for years? Let them think he'd had an accident, he didn't care.

In the restaurant, the waiter appeared not to notice even such an eye-catching character as Herr Arnold. Arnold smashed a salt cellar with a heavy knife handle, and with the silent, injured demeanor of a great tyrant, accepted the cringing apologies of the florid restaurant manager.

Afterward he drank mocha, to combat his tiredness. And even then, when he walked out, he found himself fighting sleep, which came over him with the tenacity of an old habit.

Herr Arnold strode rapidly through the unfamiliar streets, as though to get to some destination. With every step, bitter and close to tears, he sensed how insignificant he was. A man walks through the world, through his own country, his homeland for which he has worked his fingers to the bone for forty-five years – and he's a nobody. He needs to look out for cars and carts. The rascally police look sneeringly down at us. People from the lower orders, drunk and in rags, fail to make room for us. Deliverymen with boxes and bundles collide with us. Sixteen-year-olds with the faces of grown men ask us for a light. Not that we would dream of stopping to do a kindness to those snot-noses. With every step we see the corrosive tendencies of the age. This godforsaken modern age!

Dusk fell quickly over the world. The first streetlights started to glow. A cripple got in Arnold's way. He wore inflammatory proclamations on his front and back. 'Comrades,' he read, 'the plight of the war-wounded is dire! The government is sitting on its hands!' And so on and so forth. There was another fine shower! Beggars, thieves, and housebreakers. Most of them weren't even real. Faked their conditions. Playacted at being cripples! What a bunch. And the government fell for it. Writing 'Comrades!' on placards in the public street! Vile word. Anarchists. Corrosive. It smelled of bombs. Russian Jews come up with that kind of talk. The policeman stood by and did nothing. And that's what a man pays his taxes for! Terrible! And there it is, their meeting place! See them pouring into it. Strikingly few cripples among them. Three or four blind men with dogs. And apart from that – layabouts, panhandlers, scum.

It was getting late. Time to go home. Best get on a tram.

Had Herr Arnold caught a taxi home, as he surely could have done, he might have escaped the last excitement of this frightful day, and his path would not so fatefully have crossed that of the hurdy-gurdy man, Andreas Pum. But such is the treacherous way of Fate: we are doomed not by our own fault, and sometimes without our even perceiving a connection; we are doomed by the blind rage of a stranger with whose story we are unfamiliar, to whose misfortune we are unconnected, and with whose opinions we are even in agreement. He and no other is the instrument in the casually devastating hand of Destiny.

Chapter 8

IT TRANSPIRED THAT, having left his hurdy-gurdy at home, and his donkey in its shelter, as he did every Wednesday, Andreas suddenly felt so tired that, though frugal by nature and not far from home, he boarded a tram. Standing hard by the entrance, and occupying half the running board, was Herr Arnold plus umbrella, like a guard. Several other passengers had already got annoyed with the sizable gentleman, so arrogantly impeding ingress and egress. Arnold, though – and we know why – was not in the frame of mind to treat his fellow men with fairness and compassion. He, on all other occasions a supporter of order on public conveyances, was in revolt against his own convictions.

Andreas Pum had not traveled by tram for some time. He had fond feelings toward it as a mode of transport. Two or three passengers would all get up at once and offer him their seats. His crutches, his uniform that he still wore on weekdays, and his brightly polished cross all appealed to the conscience of people, even those grumpy individuals who go through life apparently the victims of a thousand injustices, with the express aim of making life worse for all they encounter. On trams, Andreas Pum always seemed to meet kindly, helpful faces.

The greater was his astonishment at this gentleman,

who did not budge an inch, even though he could see that Andreas, with crutch and stick, needed the whole width of the running board to climb up. People were milling about behind Andreas. The conductor happened to be somewhere inside the carriage. And all the while Herr Arnold looked straight ahead, seemingly oblivious to what was going on, and thinking roughly as follows:

There's one of those invalids. A simulant, of course. His other leg is just tucked up behind him. A soldier – don't make me laugh! I've seen them before. They don't even stop at dishonoring the uniform. A medal, too! The godless trickery of it! He'll have come out of that invalids' meeting I just saw. Those comrades! Not enough is done for them, they say. I'm on the Welfare Committee of the Silver Cross. Herr Reschovsky is, too. All the men in my circle are. Each of us does his bit. And they're not happy. There's gratitude for you. That bitch I barely laid a finger on yesterday sics her pimp on to me. An artiste, oh ho! He insults me. And the courts are capable of taking his side. The courts nowadays! Is there any justice left in the world?

A man's thoughts are swifter than lightning, and a brain in turmoil is capable of producing an entire revolution in the space of half a minute. The tram had been waiting for a minute already. Finally, Andreas Pum decided he would have to try and squeeze past the ossified gentleman. With the help of a woman behind him, he was successful. But now even our gentle Andreas became irritable. He refused to proceed into the carriage. He took up a position next to the immobile gentleman.

It was the first time in Andreas's life that he had taken a dislike to the face of a well-dressed gentleman. He saw the crooked nose and the reddish mustache. He had long since come to terms with his own condition – it barely occurred to him to feel indignant that there were people who weren't missing a leg. But the physical intactness of this particular gentleman now offended Andreas. It was as though he had only now discovered that he was a cripple, and others were able-bodied.

A large lady stood opposite Herr Arnold. She wore a short cloak over her little jacket, and held her hands clasped in front of her. She had a long, yellow face, a pince-nez over a diminutive nose with parchmenty nostrils. She looked like a drying bulrush.

Herr Arnold suddenly turned to her: 'These invalids are dangerous simulants. I've just come from their meeting. They're Bolsheviks to a man. I heard a speaker telling them what to do. They may look like they're halt and blind, but take it from me, they're not. It's all a trick.'

The thin lady nodded her head and attempted a smile. It resembled a lemon being pressed: painful to behold. 'The one-legged ones,' Herr Arnold went on, 'aren't really one-legged either. It's easy, you just do this!' And Herr Arnold pulled back one of his feet, to show how you conceal half a leg.

Andreas suddenly shouted out: 'You fat slob, you!'

He had no idea where that cry had come from. Never in his life had he shouted like that; even five minutes earlier it wouldn't have crossed his mind that he would assault a complete stranger and a gentleman in this way. An inexplicable hatred had its way with Andreas. Perhaps it had been in him a long time, buried beneath humility and respect.

Herr Arnold raised his hand: 'You cheat, you simulant, you Bolshevik, you!' he screamed, and a few passengers rushed out of the carriage to see what was going on.

Unfortunately, the carriage was full of petty bourgeois and women, people who had been intimidated and oppressed by the events of the revolution, but were still engaged in an embittered battle with the present. With gritted teeth, and gulping down tears, they looked back at the shining past of their country. To them the word 'Bolshevik' meant more or less thief and murderer. To them it was as though a member of their family had cried for help when he shouted: Bolshevik!

'A simulant! A Bolshevik! A Russian! A spy!' came a confusion of cries.

And a distinguished gentleman, who had remained seated in the carriage in a winter coat of signal cleanliness and shining age, muttered to himself: 'I expect it's a Jew!'

Andreas had picked up his stick, half in order to defend himself if attacked, but half in order to attack. The conductor arrived, carefully shutting his money pouch, because he knew from experience that every crowd contained a few pick-pockets, and he joined the agitated throng of passengers on the platform. The tram was just going down a long quiet street with few stops. The conductor tried to send everyone back inside the carriage. He thought for a moment which party was more likely to be in the right, and he remembered reading something in the paper, which said that simulants were wily fellows, and that a man might make thousands in the course of a day's panhandling. He still vividly felt the indignation he felt then, to learn of the brazenness of the beggars and their huge takings, which he compared with his own starvation wages. In addition, the form and features of the gentleman who was shouting reminded him of a senior magistrate he had seen once. At the same time, he remembered the bad luck of one of his colleagues who had once spoken rudely to a gentleman on his tram, and had found himself out of a job. That gentleman had been a magistrate, too. All these considerations caused the conductor to ask Andreas Pum for his papers.

Any other time, Andreas would have happily produced his permit, as he had often been asked to do by policemen to prove he was entitled to play and hobble around on his crutches to his heart's content. But right now he didn't want to. In the first place, a conductor wasn't a representative of the law; secondly he thought of himself as more than a conductor anyway; and thirdly the gentleman should have been required to show his papers first. While Andreas hesitated, the conductor thought the feigning invalid was trying to make a fool of him. So he shouted: 'Get on with it, will you!'

Andreas had never been spoken to in those tones by a conductor before. And so he said: 'I don't see why I should have to take instructions from you!'

'Then get off my tram!' ordered the conductor.

'What if I refuse?' retorted Andreas.

'Get off my tram!' shouted the conductor, and his nose went blue. And he blew a piercing blast on his whistle, which caused the driver to bring the tram to a shuddering stop.

'I'm not getting off!' said Andreas.

The conductor seized Andreas by the arm. Herr Arnold reached out for his opponent's other arm. Andreas blindly started striking out with his stick. He couldn't see a thing; red flames were circling in front of his eyes. He made contact with Herr Arnold's ear and the conductor's cap. The women fled inside the carriage. People assembled on the pavement. From their midst, as by a miracle, they suddenly produced a policeman. He parted the crowds with his arms, like a swimmer. He reached the running board and ordered: 'Come down!'

Andreas gradually calmed down when he saw the man in blue, to whom, by grace of his permit, his outlook, and his medal, he felt related. In the confident expectation that he was now in the shelter of justice, he said to the policeman: 'Ask him to come down first!' – and he pointed at Herr Arnold.

That immediately cost Andreas any sympathy he might have had from the policeman. For the man vested with absolute authority on the public streets doesn't care to obey any lesser mortal – and to him all other mortals are lesser – even though they might be one thousand times in the right. The policeman shot back:

'I don't take orders from you! In the name of the law! Get down!'

When the policeman said 'In the name of the law,' a shudder of awe went through all the participants and onlookers. Andreas had a vision of a crucifix between two burning candles, and the pale features of a judge in a mortarboard. He climbed down onto the street right away.

'Your papers,' said the policeman.

Andreas showed him his permit. Thereupon the policeman questioned the conductor, who seemed to be ignorant of the cause of the disturbance. He said nothing of its beginnings. For him the case had only begun to be interesting from the moment when Andreas had refused to follow his entirely justified demand. 'I know what the rules say,' the conductor concluded his report.

At that moment, Herr Arnold called down: 'He's a Bolshevik, I heard his rantings at the veterans' meeting!'

'You liar!' yelled Andreas, and he brandished his stick again. The policeman grabbed him by the throat. Crazy with pain and rage, Andreas struck him. A couple of bystanders wrestled his stick away from him, and he collapsed onto the pavement.

The official pulled him up with a jolt, straightened his

uniform, tucked the permit in his notebook, and his notebook in his pocket, and left the scene.

The tram went on its way, the crowd dispersed.

Andreas hobbled home.

He was still seething. He felt ashamed. He was bitterly disappointed. How could something like that happen to him! To him, Andreas Pum, who had been decorated by the government! He had a permit, he had lost a leg, and been given a cross. He was a soldier, a fighter!

Then he remembered that he didn't have his permit anymore. All at once he felt he was alive, but without any authority to live. He was nothing anymore! As if he had been thrown overboard into a great sea, his soul would thrash about desperately like a drowning man, each time he went out with his hurdy-gurdy.

He got home, and explained everything to his wife. On his way back, a frail hope had sounded in his agitated spirits, the hope in the prudence, kindness, and love of his wife.

But as he talked to her, he felt colder and colder. She said nothing. She stood in front of him, her hands on her big hips, a bunch of keys hanging down on the left like a weapon, and with dough clinging to her fingers. He couldn't see her face, he wasn't sure what impression his words were making on her. He had a feeling that she was looking down at him a little mockingly.

He ventured a quick peek up at her, and at that moment he resembled a dog expecting blows. Then his expression changed, because he was shocked. Suddenly he felt the woman standing in front of him was a complete stranger, who terrified him. Andreas discovered that a human face can look completely different when viewed from beneath. First, he saw the double chin of his wife, and then immediately above it, as though her mouth and lips no longer existed, alternately flaring out and collapsing, her capacious nostrils, from which came a damp and steamy aroma, oddly reminiscent of venison. She emitted soft growling sounds, like those from the hungry gullet of a wild animal, slavering when it sights prey.

Andreas was terrified of his wife.

He broke off his explanation. Katharina took a step away from him, and he felt himself collapsing, getting smaller and smaller, while he saw his wife bulking in front of him like a huge church tower that, when you're very close to it, you sense more than you see.

Her bosom rose and fell, and she was panting. For a few seconds, she struggled for breath and the right words. Then she found them!

'Wretched cripple!' she screeched.

Andreas turned pale. He was swimming in a vast ocean. He clutched at a chair as he might at a loose plank. As he went under, he was just able to glimpse through the fog the distant face of little Anni, who had wandered into the room to see what was going on.

Frau Katharina seemed to be oblivious of everything. She didn't see her husband or her child. She had forgotten there were such things as neighbors. Her right hand chopped through the air and upset a painted plaster vase that had been standing in the middle of the table. The water drained out of it, gurgling, and fell in single melancholy drops from the edge of the oilcloth cover onto the floor. Even better! thought Katharina. The trickling water redoubled her fury.

'That's what I get for taking you in!' she screamed. 'You go around, you live off my labor, yes, the labor of my hands, you pick fights with complete strangers and gentlemen at that, and you lose your permit. Have you gone mad? I could have had ten able-bodied men for each finger, instead of you, a wretch who is no protection and no joy, and is now a disgrace to boot. You'll be locked up, you'll be put in a cell on bread and water, and I bear your name.'

And Frau Katharina spat three times. Once she hit her husband's trousers. Trembling, Andreas wiped away his wife's spittle with the back of his hand.

Only then did Katharina turn to domestic matters. She got down on her knees, and started wiping the floor with a squeaking rag. All the while she was shouting: 'Anni, pick up the vase!' and 'Get along with you!' and 'That's my reward!' and 'Wretched cripple!'

She scrubbed and raved away at the yellow floorboards, now completely dry and gleaming. She drove her nails in between the cracks, and flicked up little scraps of dirt. Though working hard, she was able to think and even to indulge her self-pity. Stretched out on the floor, working away at it vengefully, she thought sadly of her wasted life. Oh, she thought of the trim, elegant Deputy Inspector of Police, Vinzenz Topp, whom she had turned down in favor of a cripple. Oh, what had she been thinking of!

She quickly stood up, quickly took off her apron, tossed her keys down on the table, picked up a comb, and fixed her hair. Then she slammed the door after her, and ran down the corridor to the apartment of the plumber, Fassbend, from whom the Deputy Inspector rented a tiny furnished room.

Vinzenz Topp had been on duty the previous night. He was just shaving. He went to the door with his face half lathered.

'Excuse me, excuse me, please excuse me!' said Vinzenz Topp, as he ushered Frau Katharina into his room. The Fassbends had gone to the country for a couple of days for a christening in the family of an uncle who was a farmer. Vinzenz Topp bade Frau Katharina sit down, and asked for permission to continue shaving. Politeness was second nature to him; if you'd woken him up in the middle of the night, he would have been polite.

Frau Katharina had come for legal advice. She trusted him as much as if he'd been a lawyer. Quickly and with a cool precision unusual in her sex, she related the whole episode.

Vinzenz Topp bit his lower lip as he dabbed his sore chin with the styptic pencil. Then he sprinkled some scented powder over his face. He picked his uniform jacket off the chair back and carefully slipped into it, cracking his shoulder joints. Now he was ready to give information.

It was by no means the first time that people – 'laymen,' he called them – had come to him for advice and information. He had picked up this and that from work. The case seemed very complicated to him.

'That constitutes armed resistance to the authority of the State, and insulting behavior as well. Your husband' – Vinzenz made a point of always referring to him as 'your husband,' because he was a better class of person – 'will be lucky to get off with a fine. I would say legal proceedings are on the cards, too.'

Katharina spread her arms, propped them on the table, and let her head hang. After a while she could be heard sobbing. Her arms lay there, pink, plump, and enticing.

Vinzenz Topp placed his fragrant hand on one of these arms. 'Be comforted!' he said. Then he walked over to the door and, just in case, bolted it.

Katharina lifted her tear-bedewed face. She wasn't sure if she was crying for her husband or Vinzenz Topp. He was so lovely with his white powdered face and his smell of nice toilet soap. His uniform fitted him like a glove. What had she been thinking of?

She made comparisons. It was inevitable.

'Save me!' she suddenly sobbed out, throwing open her arms. Vinzenz launched himself into them.

And so he came to enjoy the woman he had long and secretly lusted after. Fortune had smiled on him.

He didn't omit to level grave accusations against Andreas, no longer referring to him as 'your husband.' He made mild reproaches to Frau Katharina, too. But it was all in a tender, superior, joshing tone that Katharina had never heard before.

By the time she left his room, it was late in the evening. She smelled of his soap, she joyfully carried his scent around with her. It may be said that that evening she was completely happy.

Chapter 9

ANDREAS PUM'S MISFORTUNE had benefited someone else, too, namely Herr Arnold. His rage had evaporated. He tried to forget the disagreeable Luigi Bernotat. He would go and see his lawyer tomorrow. He kissed his wife and his two blooming children. He had more kind words for the maid. And, even though there was a certain severity in his manner, his words and his gestures, those around him did breathe a little more easily. He cast a friendly shadow on his family.

Meanwhile, Andreas Pum went to his shelter. There stood his Mooli, radiating warmth. A bat was hibernating in a nook between two posts. The damp straw stank, and near the door it was actually frozen. The wind blew through the hinges. Through a crack, Andreas could see a few stars in the winter night. He fiddled with a straw. Then he twisted a ring out of three straws and set it on Mooli's ear. It was a friendly animal that liked being stroked. Slowly and tenderly it raised a rear hoof, and it looked as though it were trying in its clumsy way to stroke Andreas. There was enough light to see its eyes. They were big in the dark and amber-yellow. They were damp, as though filled with sadness, but still reluctant to cry.

The more the night advanced, the colder it became. Andreas felt like whimpering, but he felt too ashamed to do so in front of the animal. His missing leg hurt him again, for the first time in a long time. He unbuckled his leg, and felt his stump. It had the shape of a flattened cone. The flesh was crisscrossed with faint cracks and hollows. When Andreas put his hand on it, the pain eased. But the other pain in his heart was unappeasable.

It was a still, bright night. Dogs barked. Doors banged in the dark. The snow creaked, even with no one walking about on it, merely because of the wind. The world outside seemed to be expanding. He could see only a tiny scrap of sky through a chink. But it was enough to give a clear taste of infinity.

Did God live beyond the stars? Could He bear to watch a man's misery and not intervene? What went on behind that icy blue? Was the world ruled by a tyrant, whose injustice was as boundless as the heavens themselves?

Why does He punish us with His sudden disfavor? We've done nothing wrong, we've not even sinned in our thoughts. Quite the opposite: we were always pious and devoted to Him, though we didn't know Him, and if our lips didn't praise Him every single day, we still lived contentedly, and without wicked resentments in our breast, modest links in the chain of the world, as He created it. Did we give Him occasion to avenge Himself on us? To change the world so much that everything that seemed good to us about it, suddenly turned bad? Or did He perhaps know of a secret sin within us, of whose existence we ourselves were unaware?

And so Andreas began looking for hidden sins in his soul, with the urgency of someone looking through his pockets for his missing wristwatch. But he found none. Was it a sin that he had married the widow Blumich, and was her dead husband now avenging himself? Oh, did the dead live? Had he sinned against Mooli, the donkey, ever? Had it been wrong of him, on the occasions when Mooli had stopped and looked for something or other on the ground, that he had sometimes given the donkey a gentle tap to get it going once more? And had it always been nothing more than a gentle tap? Not a hard, pitiless, brutal blow? 'Mooli, my donkey!' whispered Andreas, and he pressed his cheek against the animal's flank.

Toward morning, Andreas fell asleep. The early sounds of traffic were already audible. The animal was still. It grunted softly and wet the straw, which straightaway froze. Its urine smelled heavy and ammoniac.

The following morning, Andreas walked into the apartment without a word. He helped himself to bread and margarine from the cupboard. Little Anni came home from school. She pressed herself against him, as though in appeasement. 'Play something!' she said. And Andreas played the most sorrowful tunes the manufacturer had supplied for the instrument, 'The Boy Sat by the Fountain' and 'Lorelei.' The tunes reminded him of that happy summer's day when he'd first set foot in the courtyard.

And what a wonderful summer it had been, a precious string of happy days, days of freedom and sunshine, the ancient linden trees standing in the welcoming courtyards. The windows had flown open on every story, the girls had stuck their round, red, joyful faces out of the kitchen windows like jolly paper lanterns, and the smells of cooking had filled his nostrils. Laughing children had danced around to the music, his cross had twinkled in the sun, his uniform, today bedraggled with dung and straw, how clean and impressive it had looked then!

Katharina came in. She bustled about, with short, practical movements. She seemed not to have noticed the presence of her husband. Without a word, she banged down an earthenware dish in front of him. He knew that little dish with its cracked glaze. Sometimes old beggars, or stray cats and dogs were fed from it. Katharina herself ate her soup from a red-rimmed china plate. Also, she'd kept her potatoes and her cabbage apart. On Andreas's little dish, everything was all mixed up, and a large bone stuck out of the mess like a broken rooftree from the ruins of a house.

What should he do? He ate, and grew humble, and from time to time looked at Katharina. She had a red face, and her hair had been very carefully marcelled, with lots of tiny curls on either side of her face, and in the middle a row of straight bangs combed down and cut with a sharp ruler, that looked like the tassels of a shawl. She smelled like a hairdresser's salon, of all kinds of things, patchouli and hair tonic and cologne. Any other man would have known at once that she had spent the entire morning at the hairdresser's. Andreas noticed nothing.

He was preoccupied instead by the riddle of the sudden changes that had taken place around him. It was as if by magic. He tried to remember the incident in the tram clearly. He saw the gentleman who had attacked him. Or had it perhaps been the other way round? What was it the gentleman had said? That invalids simulated? He was quite right! Andreas had often seen such simulants himself. Why had he taken the gentleman's remarks personally? He had been generalizing. He was quite rightly incensed at the meeting. They were a band of scroungers, rebels, and atheists, they wanted to topple the government, and they deserved whatever was coming to them.

It was just an exception, Andreas had been unlucky enough to encounter a hostile conductor and an unsympathetic policeman. Just let him appear in court. There he will call for the condign punishment of these low-grade officials. He will present his C.V., his part in the War, his love of God and country. He will have his permit restored to him. He will regain Katharina's respect. He will be the master in his own house. A husband to his wife. She stood up. Her broad hips, squeezed into their corset, seemed to move independently, and the bursting fullness of her breasts wobbled with every step. Andreas thought about their nights of love, the pressure of her yielding but muscular thighs, and he cupped his hands and thought he could feel the broad, burgeoning, limitless softness of her breasts again.

Oh, just give us our day in court! There, there are no uncultivated policemen and no unmannerly tram conductors. Justice sheds its light over the courts. Sapient, distinguished men in gowns look deeply into the hearts of men, and with careful hands they sift the wheat from the chaff.

If Andreas had known anything of jurisprudence, he would have known that the courts were already busy with his case. For his was one of the so-called 'express cases,' which, following a decree from the progressive Minister of Justice, were picked up and dealt with right away. The great grinding wheels of the State were getting to grips with the citizen Andreas Pum, and, before he even realized it, he was being slowly and comprehensively crushed.

Chapter 10

THE FOLLOWING MORNING, a legal summons arrived for 'Permit-holder Andreas Pum.' It bore an official seal, a white lithographed eagle on a round red ground, and although the address had been hastily scrawled – proof, if proof were needed, of the pressure on the legal system – the missive still communicated something of the slow pomp that characterizes our great institutions. It was a summons to the 2nd Chamber, which dealt with pressing minor cases. For the first time, Andreas Pum found himself described as 'the accused,' a word that, coming from a court of law, is little short of 'the guilty party.' Beyond that, the document gave only the date and place of the hearing; another, pale and somewhat smudged, version of the seal; and the illegible signature of a magistrate, which suggested that the official wished to preserve his anonymity.

Andreas perused the summons several times, in a foolish and unrealistic hope that he might be able to glean something between the lines, whether to his advantage or not, some clue as to the official's mood. When that failed, he tried to visualize the court, the crucifix, the lights, the railing, the dock, the public defendant, the magistrate, the recorder, the usher, the stacks of files, and the big painting of the Lord, to whom he was already addressing silent prayers. He walked over to the yellow brick church, for the first time since his wedding. It was empty, one high window was open, and winter sent its chilly breath into the house of God, which still had a musty smell of people, of snuffed candles and whitewash. Andreas folded his hands, knelt down, and in the reedy voice with which he'd prayed as a boy before school, he recited the Lord's Prayer, three, four, five times.

Thereupon he felt calmer, proofed against unpleasant surprises, against the judgment that the morrow would bring.

He went home, where there was a stranger in the room. The man stood up and bowed slightly, sat down again, and said to Andreas: 'I'm just waiting for your wife. Excuse me! She'll be here within the quarter hour. Your wife called on me in my business earlier. You see what a punctual man I am. On the road all day, and always punctual, that's my watchword.'

Andreas looked at the man with hostility, though he neither knew him nor understood him. He was certainly there for some evil purpose – Andreas could sense that. For a while he tried to guess what the stranger's business and intentions might be – but he couldn't. As long as the stranger remained seated, he gave the impression of being a tall man, but when he stood up he was actually very small. He was short in the legs. His little potbelly argued a certain cheerfulness, as did his red girlish cheeks and the innocent little black mustache and smooth, clean-shaven, powdered chin, with a smiling dimple in the middle of it. His nose too was a delicate, trifling little thing, as though molded from plaster of paris. But in his little black eyes there was an evil gleam. The stranger looked like a chubby boy with the size, manner, voice, and beard of a man. He gave off a blithe wickedness, a malign cheerfulness. He sat there, and didn't even look as though he was waiting.

He didn't appear bored for a moment. His glowing eyes shot sparks over the items in the room, the carpet, the doilies, the blue stoneware vase, the embroidered cushion, as though to incinerate it all. There he sat, entirely absorbed, showing that his lively mind was able to find interest in the most indifferent things in the world.

Still aromatic, still in a cloud of perfumed frivolity, Frau Katharina walked in, and the man leaped to his feet as though he'd been stung. 'And a very good evening to you, ma'am,' he said. 'Let's get straight down to business. Delay never pays! That's my watchword.'

Katharina jangled her keys. Andreas watched her and the man quietly from his corner. He followed them when they went outside. There was cold sweat on his brow, and his heart was pounding irregularly, with great beats that threatened to smash his rib cage. Leaning against the door onto the courtyard, he stood and watched as his wife opened Mooli's shelter and led the donkey out. It was a dry, sunny day, and the little animal cast an improbably large shadow across the glittering snow. The world grew dark before Andreas's eyes. The radiant sky turned dark blue and seemed to come down like a curtain. The color of everything was dark green, as though seen through a beer bottle. Everything happened in that magical, dreamy illumination. The stranger patted the donkey. He gave it a pinch, as though to gauge the thickness of its hide. He tickled the tips of its ears, till it turned its head and gave a little shudder.

'Now, ma'am,' said the stranger, 'what good do you think an animal like that is to me? I'm not saying I can't do anything with it, but what good is it to me? Now if it had been a little horse, or even a pony . . .' he said fondly, as though speaking to a foal himself.

'But I told you it was a donkey,' replied Frau Katharina, in a shrill and determined voice that did not bode well.

'Yes, yes,' said the man, with lowered eyes, 'a donkey, of course. But such a little one!'

'But a donkey's not a camel!' cried Frau Katharina.

'Madam is joking now, ha, ha, yes of course a donkey's a donkey. But there are large ones and small ones, and even some tiny ones. Believe me, I've seen them tinier than this!'

'Well then!' crowed Katharina. 'You said it yourself!'

The man reached slowly for his wallet. He pulled out three banknotes that were crisp and new, counted them twice, held them up in the air, and went on rustling them awhile longer.

Then he looped his fat little arm around Mooli, and the beast trotted off, past Andreas. Katharina looked straight through him, as though he were just a part of the door frame.

Andreas watched his donkey as far as the door. The man looked back over his shoulder and said: 'Good evening, ma'am.'

Andreas hobbled after him. He watched them all the way down the street. There was the man with Mooli trotting beside him, on the very edge of the pavement, next to the curb, the dear beast, the warm lovely creature. Its eyes had been golden brown, and inside its gray body there dwelt a human soul.

Chapter 11

THE DAY ANDREAS was due in court dawned like an ordinary day, like every other day that had preceded it. During the night, which Andreas had spent on the sofa, in his clothes and without a pillow, he had come up with a brilliant speech, which would infallibly result in his being asked for forgiveness, and the gentleman, the policeman, and the conductor all being thrown in prison. Andreas felt calm that morning. His hearing was at ten o'clock. It was almost certain that by twelve Andreas Pum would leave the court building victorious and in possession of his permit.

The sun was a little warmer by now, and the frost was broken. The snow began to thaw. The roofs dripped with a sweet, optimistic melody. Yes, a sparrow even began to twitter. The clemency of nature was like God's forgiveness.

Andreas would not have set any store by such signs, if he had known a little more about the law. He didn't know that the well-oiled wheels of its machinery occasionally – especially in minor cases – moved independently of one another, each one working individually in order to grind into dust the victim they had been given by chance. For not only the Courts, but also the Police are entitled to levy fines, and anyone who tangles with the Police must first be dealt with by them. It was the view of the Police that Andreas was guilty of a common 'violation' and was therefore no longer worthy of holding the permit he had been given by special dispensation of the State. So Andreas Pum needed first of all to be taken in for questioning.

And so it happened that, while he was getting ready to go to Court, the door opened and a policeman walked in to take Andreas to his police questioning. In his catastrophic ignorance of the various organs of the state, Andreas supposed the policeman had come on the Court's business, and told him the hearing wasn't until ten o'clock. The officer asked to see the summons, expertly explained to Andreas the enormous difference, twirled his blond mustaches, and finally said: 'Well, I've got to do my duty!' That meant he had no choice but to fulfill his task of taking Andreas to the Police. He advised Andreas to show his summons to the Police Inspector.

Andreas calmed down. He still had a sense of some new impending calamity. But common sense told him that the State must take responsibility for its own errors, and surely the citizen had the right to draw the authorities' attention to their own contradictions. And so he went. On the way, he told the friendly law officer the whole story. The man laughed heartily and loudly, his blue eyes sparkled, and his strong white teeth shone. 'You've nothing to fear!' he said. And Andreas took heart.

At the police station he was made to wait. Either the official who was going to question him hadn't arrived yet, or else he was busy with someone else. The clock on the bare office wall showed half past nine. Andreas stumped up to the barrier, behind which a man in uniform was copying names and numbers from yellow filing cards onto red ones, and said: 'Excuse me!'

The officer went on with what he was doing. He was on K. He didn't want to be interrupted. Not until he turned the page and got to L did he raise his head.

Andreas showed him his summons. The officer asked what it was he'd done now, as though he'd already been through some severe disappointments with him. Andreas related the incident in minute detail. There were a couple of prostitutes waiting in the room. They laughed.

The officer folded the summons and said: 'Wait a minute!' And he wrote some more. Finally a door opened, and a voice called out: 'Andreas Pum!' Andreas walked up to the gentleman and bowed, at which his crutch slipped out from under him a little, and he caught himself with his hand on the desk behind which the inspector was seated.

'Now, now!' he exclaimed.

'I beg your pardon,' stammered Andreas. 'I have a summons!'

'I know that,' replied the gentleman. 'Please don't speak unless I ask you a question.'

Thereupon he began reading the report of the policeman who had booked Andreas. When he got to the place where the permit was mentioned, he turned it around slightly, so that Andreas could read it, too.

'Is that right?' asked the Inspector.

He was a young man with a very high stiff collar and a very small thin face. His pointy chin threatened to disappear into his collar. His voice was squeaky. And all the while, he was smoothing down his hair with both hands, and with his fingertips softly checking the straightness of his parting.

'Yes,' said Andreas, 'but not quite.'

'What do you mean?' asked the Inspector.

Andreas told his story for the third time. Then he quickly

pulled out his summons and showed it to the Inspector. He looked up at the clock and said: 'Too late! Why didn't you say so right away?'

'What shall I do now?' asked Andreas.

'We'll take care of this first.'

'How long will that take?'

'That's no concern of yours!' screamed the Inspector. 'No concern of yours,' he repeated – and he leaped to his feet. He began pacing back and forth. He banged on his desk and shouted: 'Infernal cheek!'

Andreas could feel the blood rushing into his face. Hatred of the official seized him and shook him so that he trembled. He banged his crutch on the ground. His mouth was full of saliva. He spat.

The official clenched his fists. Andreas saw him distantly. The official was yelling. Andreas heard a soft, muffled version of his rant. There were red wheels swirling in front of him. He lifted his stick and struck a lamp shade. It shattered into smithereens. Two men hurled themselves upon him.

'Twenty-four hours!' screamed the official. Then he handed Andreas Pum's file to a secretary: 'Permit withdrawn!' he sighed, and: 'Next!'

And as Andreas was led across the yard to the prison for petty criminals, all the thoughts vanished from his head. It was as if his skull had been drained. There was a painful void in his head.

Chapter 12

THE CELLS SEEMED to be a long way underground, because Andreas tumbled into the half dark. He stopped by the cell door. He heard the crunch of the key. He felt dead. The sun was extinguished. The days had finally run out, irretrievably scattered like a broken string of pearls. Life would not return. It was finished. There was nothing left. His eyes were dead. A curtain was drawn over everything they had ever seen and dwelled on. Behind them were the fading images of things, animals, people. Mooli, the little donkey, died on the street corner where it disappeared from sight. A plump rosy Death had bought the animal and strangled it with its short round arm. Katharina is dead, his Kathi, the broad-hipped, high-breasted woman. Anni, the little girl with the thin pigtail, is dead. The big, white, broad-winged ribbon was a vampire on the child's head. Wiped out as with a big sponge, as if they'd been nothing but a child's drawing on the blackboard, are the hospital, the War, the permit, his comrades, Engineer Lang, Willi, his girlfriend, the hurdy-gurdy, the tram. They wafted through his memory in frail, perished outlines.

His lumberyard loomed out of the half dark of the cell, as though smeared on a canvas by the rapid brushstrokes of a ghostly painter. There is Castor, the scruffy dog with his luminous green eyes that glow in the dark, his pompous bushy tail that always seemed to be raised in admonishment like a fatherly index finger, his padding gait that was like a walk on the carpet of the darkness. There was the perimeter fence, painted brown and smelling of creosote, topped by a triple row of wire, with little spikes and prongs like a row of iron teeth. The moon rises behind a pile of boards and climbs over some protruding laths to pour itself out over the yard and gild the sawdust that lies softly on the ground. And Andreas makes his rounds, keys and weapons jingling, the dog at his heels, beside him, in front of him. When he's tired, he lies down, resting his back against the fence, and his tired eyes gaze down over his belly, his knees, his toe caps.

When he hears a sound, then the dog growls and he slowly gets to his feet, clutching his weapons and keys, and like a stalking animal moves one foot at a time, one foot at a time, and his boots don't creak the way they usually do, because his feet force them to remain silent.

He was a good night watchman, Andreas Pum. He should have remained one.

But he lost a leg.

He lost a piece of himself and carried on living.

It is possible to lose an important, valuable, indispensable part of oneself and carry on living. You walk on two legs, then you lose half of one below the knee, like the blade of a penknife, and you walk on. It doesn't hurt, there's no blood, there was no flesh there, no bone, no veins. Was it wood? A crutch? A natural crutch? Better put together than an artificial one, as silent as rubber and as strong as steel?

You could walk silently or with a noisy stride. You could stamp with either foot. You could hop. You could hold your foot in your hand. You could do knee bends, quick ones or all the way down. You could exercise.

All that we can no longer do, and some other things besides.

How long has it been that we could no longer set one foot silently in front of the other? Each one of our strides resounds and echoes. Our approach is noisy, and our going away is a clatter. We are forever surrounded by din. The crutch punches holes in our thoughts. People on two legs overtake us.

The two-legged are our enemies. The gentleman on the platform with the squishy nose has two legs. The rowdy conductor has two legs. The disrespectful policeman has two legs. The police inspector with the pointy chin has two legs. Katharina has two legs. The apple-cheeked Death who called for Mooli has two legs. All the 'heathens' have two legs.

Andreas himself has become a heathen. He has got himself arrested. He has had his permit taken away. He has, in all innocence, become a heathen. Would he be in the cell otherwise?

There are others beside himself in this spacious cell: No doubt they are murderers, infidels, crooks.

But they are also heathens, like Andreas. He doesn't hate them. Unlike them, he hasn't stolen, but he has lost his god.

It is possible to lose one's god. God was perhaps in his knee joint.

'What are you standing for?' asked a man who was sitting on an upturned chest.

'There's lots of room here for the quality!'

Andreas sat down.

'Are you an invalid?' asked the man.

'Yes!'

'What's that bit of metal on your chest for?'

'I don't know.'

They fall silent. From the depths of the cell, a croaky drunkard's voice calls out: 'Got any cigarettes?'

'Yes!'

A form emerged from the gloom, and swam closer, parting the darkness.

There were three of them. Andreas had five cigarettes. They decided to share them.

'You new here?' said Croaky.

'Give us that metal!' shouted another.

The third walked up to Andreas, ripped the cross off his chest, and held it up in front of his face to inspect it.

'A bit of plaster to make you feel better!' he said.

'What paragraph?' asked the croaker.

He was a 'lawyer.'

One of the others translated: 'He wants to know what you're in for!'

Andreas said: 'I don't know. I shouldn't really be here at all. I've got a summons for today!' And he produced his summons.

The 'lawyer' read it. On his pants he lit a match that he carried loose in his pocket, and he read. 'You'd better get a move on, guy! What's the time?'

'It's too late,' said Andreas.

'Well, then they'll have sent you down anyway.'

'What for?'

'Because you weren't there. The court's got nothing to do with the police, and the police has got nothing to do with the courts. If you're the accused, and you don't attend your hearing, they'll tell you your sentence starts tomorrow. What was it you did?'

Andreas described the incident on the tram.

'Well, now,' said Croaky, 'that might come under threatening behavior to an official. Insulting behavior for sure. Maybe resisting arrest. If the officials say you struck them, the court will say: violent criminal! Six weeks! You should have gone!'

'But they brought me here!'

'Then you just don't go back there. That way you won't have to do any time either. Six weeks is nothing to me. Not for you, though. What do you do for a living?'

'I've got a permit! I play the hurdy-gurdy!'

'Sell it to me!'

'I'll have to go home and get it!'

'I'll get it for you. Where d'you live? Fix up some signal with your old lady, so she can recognize me.'

'Can we talk about it tomorrow?' said Andreas.

'You're a fool,' said Croaky. 'You've done everything wrong. If I was you, I'd have sued the gentleman. You just need to know the ropes. I would have beaten him up and then sued him. What did he look like? Maybe I'll run into him sometime. The world is round and not all that big.'

But Andreas couldn't help him.

The others fell asleep. One after another, they started snoring.

Andreas wouldn't mind doing six weeks, and more. He'd like to be put away for life.

We are all of us prisoners anyway, Andreas Pum! The laws lie open like traps on the paths we poor bastards walk. Even if we have a permit, there are still always policemen lurking in the shadows. We are always trapped, and at the mercy of the State, of the two-legged ones, of the police, of gentlemen on tram platforms, of women, and of donkey-buyers.

Chapter 13

THE FOLLOWING MORNING, Andreas Pum was given a cup of coffee and a piece of bread. He said goodbye to his three friends. 'Take care you don't wind up here again!' said Croaky.

When Andreas set foot on the street outside, he felt the world had been freshly painted and renovated, he no longer felt at home in it; just as you feel like a stranger when you return to your room and it's been painted a different color. The movements of people, vehicles, and dogs were all strange and baffling to him. Particularly odd was the swarming of bicycles on a busy square, like light-colored mosquitoes in among the big buses and trams, trucks, and black-covered hackney cabs. A vibrant yellow vehicle swaggered, rattled, and surged across the square. On its side was the burning red legend: 'Smoke Iota Cigarettes.' It was the van of insanity. Insanity sat inside it, surrounded by four vibrant yellow and burning red walls, and his breath wafted destructively out of the little barred windows. Strange that it's taken me until now to see the connections, thinks Andreas. That car spreads the germ of insanity throughout the world. That car has driven past me thousands of times. How stupid of me! It was never a mail van! What would the post office be doing with Iota cigarettes? What does the post office care about what cigarettes people smoke?

Andreas stumbles upon a thousand weird and wonderful things. There's a weathervane stuck on top of a poster pillar. It performs little pirouettes, as though unable to make up its mind. If you stand in front of it and watch it, you hear it rattling quietly in the midst of all the noise of the street. What's a weathervane doing on top of a poster pillar? A sign of the general insanity? What else could it be? Is it the job of a poster pillar to indicate which way the wind's blowing? Or just to announce lectures, theater productions, and concerts?

Andreas rolled his eyes heavenward, because he wanted to get away from the madness of the world. For Heaven is of a clear and imperishable blue, its color is as pure as divine wisdom, and the clouds forever pass in front of it. But today the clouds formed distorted faces, gargoyles blew by, God was pulling faces.

Since the world had changed, Andreas decided not to bother with it anymore, and not to go back to prison.

His eye was caught by something on his chest. He remembered he wasn't wearing his cross anymore. And, needing some new kind of medal instead of the one he had been given in his old life, to correspond to his rebirth, he reflected on the word 'heathen,' a stubborn word that suddenly acquired a new meaning, and which, like a medal, he now conferred on himself.

Andreas Pum declared himself a heathen. He exuberantly reckoned himself one of the fraternity of criminals. He felt his walk become edgy and his expression shifty when a policeman passed. Like a wanted man, a killer, Andreas slunk through the side alleys of the city.

And so, without having meant to, he came to his old apartment. It was as though he had left it only yesterday. As he had always done, on account of Willi's profound sleep, he rapped on the door three times with his stick. He heard Willi's stifled yawn, and the cracking of powerful joints that always accompanied Willi's stretching.

'Well, look who it isn't!' said Willi. 'Where did you park your baby grand?'

Andreas felt vastly encouraged by the sight of Willi. He trusted him like a brother. The room was in its customary funereal twilight. A snug, familiar, stale and sour odor came off the walls and the dirty bed. And the intoxication that comes over sensitive people when, after a long journey round the world, they cross the border of their native land – that same intoxication of homecoming now filled Andreas Pum.

Willi laid the table with a piece of cardboard. Thereupon he brought the sausage, which he still procured from his old supplier on the side street. And then he poured some schnapps into a teacup.

'Yesterday was Klara's birthday!' he explained. And, with his elbows propped in front of him on the table, he sat and listened to Andreas's strange and peculiar story, which, he concluded, could only have happened to that idiot of a cripple.

'You can stay here!' Willi determined with the certainty of a man of authority, who decides things quickly. 'We'll see if they ever find you!' said Willi, and he sounded genuinely curious. And then he went back to sleep.

KLARA, TOO, LISTENED to Andreas's story with some consternation. 'So you've lost wife and child and everything!' she said, for she was a softhearted creature.

'Easy come, easy go,' said Willi. Then he sang the first verse of a popular ballad.

'I wouldn't cross the stupid Courts if I was you!' said the

softhearted but still apprehensive Klara. 'Go and serve out your six weeks.'

But Willi, opposed on principle to such concessions, gave her a push in the back that sent her sprawling across the table. That night, Andreas slept the deep, pure, smiling sleep of a baby. But in the morning two detectives came. They had failed to find him with his wife, and she had told them about his former address. They led him away. They took him to the commuter station and then quite a bit past it.

The prison lay among large fields, a big building with lots of jagged turrets of reddish-brown brick.

There it was, dominating the countryside, hallowed as a church and forbidding as the walls of the law. The last thing Andreas saw of the outside world was a little cat. Perhaps she belonged to one of the wardens. She ran along the fence that separated the house of justice from a footpath, with a tinkling bell on a red band round her neck. She reminded Andreas of a little girl.

Chapter 14

ANDREAS GOT ACCUSTOMED to his cell very quickly; its sourish damp, its penetrating cold, and the crosshatched gray that did duty for daylight. Yes, he learned to distinguish between the different phases of darkness that represented morning, noon, and night, and the foggy hours of twilight. He adapted to the darkness of the night, his eye grew able to pierce its impenetrableness, making it translucent, like a dark glass at noon. He drew the specific luminosity out of the few objects among which he lived, so that he could study them at night, and they even offered him their contours. He came to hear the voice of the darkness and the song of silent things, whose muteness begins to sound as the noisome day recedes. He could hear the sound made by a clambering wood louse when it left the smooth surface of the wall and reached a place where the plaster had crumbled off, and the bare cracked bricks were exposed. He could identify the feeble squallings of the big city that reached as far as the prison, each one after its kind, and by origin and derivation. From the tiniest distinctions in their sounds, he identified the nature and the shape and the extent of things. He knew if it was a swanky private carriage that was racing by outside or just a well-constructed cab; whether a horse had the fine limbs of a thoroughbred or the broad hooves of a more utilitarian animal; he knew the

difference between the crisp trot of the stallion that was pulling a light wagonette on silent rubber tires, and the one that
carried its gentleman rider on its back. He knew the dragging
gait of the old man and the stroll of the young nature lover;
the skippy walk of the coltish girl and the purposeful tread
of the busy mother. He could hear the difference between a
walker and a hiker, a slender frame and a heavyset one, could
tell the strong from the weak. He acquired the magical gifts of
the blind. His ear became sighted.

During his first days in prison, he still attempted to look
out through the high barred window.

He pushed his wooden bench under the window, and
wouldn't give up until with both hands he had caught the
edge of the masonry where the window bars were fitted. Oh
– he had only one leg, his blunt crutch obtained less grip on
the sheer wall than his good foot managed to find, and for
seconds he hung with all his weight from his cramping fingertips. So his body dangled suspended in the air, and his soul
between the desire to see a paltry slice of the world, and the
fear of falling back and meeting his death. Never had he been
in greater danger. For never – not even in the field – had he
had so keen a sense of the preciousness of life, the little scrap
of life that the cell left him. By cunning and thousandfold
exertion, he stole a brief moment of the world outside the
dirty glass and the bars, and still came down feeling refreshed
and enriched to the everlasting dark gray, as though he had
enjoyed all the wonders of the world. The little excursions he
took with his eyes regularly reconciled him to the implacabil-
ity of his jail; showing him that not even the cell that locked
him in was outside the world, and that he was still a part of
life. He was a cripple, not an absolute lord of the earth like a
man with two legs. He couldn't walk quietly, or hop, or run.

But at least he was able to limp, and, in six weeks, in six short weeks, he could tread the earth with one foot again.

Sometimes he hoped to see the little cat that he had met when he entered prison. But all that his eyes could take in was the edge of the dark pine wood in the distance and a narrow strip of sky; sometimes a bird; a cloud pushing past; once even the frail wings of an airplane, though he heard them often, as there was an airfield nearby. But what he longed to see was the little cat. She was what he had seen in his last moment of freedom. At night his acute hearing sometimes picked up a soft tinkling sound. He imagined it came from the bell that was tied around the cat's neck.

But soon enough he forgot about her. He no longer tried to shin up the wall. His cell became home to him. A thousand images flowered out of his solitude. A thousand voices filled it. He saw a pig that had got its snout jammed in the doorway of its sty. It was a familiar image. He had seen it when he was a boy, on the farm of his uncle who was a tax collector in the country. He saw the swallows' nest in the latrine there; the chained parrot that tried to nibble his finger; the compass and the silver-mounted tooth on his father's watch chain; the birth of a butterfly from the frail, papery sheath of the pupa in a grass-lined matchbox; dried anemones in a herbarium; a gold-deckled hymnal and his first tie, which was of red silk.

Andreas had plenty to do. He had to put these images in order. Like a child on the rungs of a ladder, the newborn Andreas scaled timidly up and down these little memories. It seemed to him that he would have to climb for a long time yet before recollecting himself. He was discovering himself. He closed his eyes and felt happy. Each time he opened them again, he had found a new piece of himself, a connection, a sound, a day, an image. He felt as though he were just starting school, and was acquiring all kinds of secret knowledge. He had spent forty-five years of his life in blindness, without knowing himself or the world.

Life must be altogether different from what he had supposed. A woman who loved him had betrayed him when he needed her. If he had known her at all, he would never have allowed it to happen. But what had he known of her? Her lips, her breasts, her flesh, her broad features, and the moist smell of her. What had he put his trust in? In God, in Justice, in the Government. He lost his leg in the war. He was decorated. They hadn't even got him an artificial leg for his trouble. For years he wore his cross with pride. His permit, which entitled him to crank the handle of a hurdy-gurdy in people's courtyards, seemed a huge reward. But one day the world turned out not to be as simple as he had supposed in his simplemindedness. The Government was unjust. It persecuted not only the murderers, the pickpockets, the heathens. Evidently it must also decorate murderers, seeing as it had locked up the decent and God-fearing Andreas, though he revered it. And God was just the same: He too made mistakes. But was God still God if He made mistakes?

Every morning the inmates went exercising in the yard. The yard was closely paved with little bricks, so there was no puff of dust, no crumb of soil in it. A big event was the hen that occasionally turned up there. One hundred and fifty-four prisoners filed along the walls in a clockwise direction. In the middle were the speckled hen and a guard who had a bamboo cane in his hand and carried a revolver at his hip. The prisoners all had numbers on their left sleeves. No. 1 was the first line, and No. 154 the last. They walked around the yard four times. Then the hour was up. They didn't speak. They gazed wistfully at the hen. Occasionally one of them grinned. No. 73 was Andreas Pum.

Once he spotted a scrap of newspaper in the yard. The guard just happened to be looking the other way. Andreas picked it up and hid it in his hand. He was intensely curious. It was like being given another human being to talk to in his cell. Perhaps, yes, probably, that piece of paper would contain something interesting or amusing. He crumpled it up and held it between two fingers. That allowed him to keep his hand flat against the seam of his trousers in the regulation way. That morning, exercise seemed to go on forever, the hour just wouldn't end, the yard seemed cruelly huge. At last the guard blew his whistle. Andreas went back to his cell, and waited for his eyes to get used to the dark. Then he unfolded his scrap of paper, moved the bench under the window, and sat down. He read:

Personal Column. The engagements are announced between Fräulein Elsbeth Waldeck, daughter of Prof. Leopold Waldeck, and Dr. med. Edwin Aronowsky; Fräulein Hildegard Goldschmidt and Dr. jur. Siegfried Türkel; Fräulein Erna Walter and Willi Reizenbaum. The bank manager Willibald Rolowsky and his wife Martha Maria, née Zadik, proudly announce the birth of a son. Frau Hedwig Kalischer, née Goldenring, mourns the passing of her husband, Leopold Kalischer, partner in the firm König, Schrumm and Kalischer, Chairman of the Association of Chemical Manufacturers, in his 62nd year, following a short illness. Herr Johann Kotz mourns the passing of his wife, Frau Helene Kotz. The mine director Harald Kreuth announces the passing of his father, Sigismund Johann Kreuth. In his 77th year, following a long illness, Dr. med. Max Treitel, Member of the Board of Health, has passed away.

Andreas turned the paper over, and read:

If this is indeed the case, it becomes clear why the Poincaré press has been so assiduous in praising the report as pro-French – to cover their master. The *Daily Mail*, citing reliable sources in Paris, has it on good authority—

And that was all.

Andreas Pum tried to imagine the people about whom he had learned certain crucial facts. Fräulein Elsbeth Waldeck was blond and posh, a Professor's daughter, engaged to a Doctor. Dr. jur. Siegfried Türkel might be an attorney, and it wouldn't hurt to make his acquaintance. If one was acquainted with Attorney Türkel, one perhaps didn't have to go to prison at all. Yes, that's how it must be: all the people who had their names on this scrap of newspaper were friends of one another. Dr. Aronowsky had Martha Maria, née Zadik, as a patient, and the Mine Director, Harald Kreuth, borrowed money from the bank manager Willibald Rolowsky. He in turn was represented in Court by Attorney Türkel, who called on Herr Johann Kotz to pay his condolences. The names leaped out of the lines and entered into different relationships with each other. The Member of the Board of Health slipped over to the Mine Director, who became the Attorney. The names were alive. They took on human form. Andreas Pum looked at his scrap of newspaper as a room, in which all these people were standing and walking and talking to one another.

The idea moved him. He imagined a very exclusive society.

He thought he had discovered the secret of the universe. He felt sure he was in his cell merely because he knew none of these engaged, newborn, or deceased parties. Why was it nowhere printed that Andreas Pum, permit-holder, after unjust treatment and his case still unheard, had been sentenced to six weeks in jail?

Chapter 15

THAT OFFENDED ANDREAS PUM. Andreas felt the humiliation of individuals who had prepared themselves for a particular career, only to be overlooked. The fact that he of all people had been locked up, and had been forced to become a heathen, was a crass, inexcusable, criminal injustice. How long ago was it now that he, with the dignity almost of a state functionary, and certainly with the God-fearing devoutness of a priest, had stood, with his permit in his pocket, on a crowded street corner, playing the National Anthem, exhorting passersby to patriotism quite as much as to charity? Since a policeman had strode up to him, only to turn on his heel with a bow, because he was compelled to recognize that Andreas Pum was fully entitled to play?

What had happened? How could the world have changed so quickly?

Ah, but it hadn't changed! It had always been that way! Only if we are especially fortunate do we manage to stay out of prison. But we are fated to cause revulsion, and to find ourselves ensnared in the luxuriant undergrowth of the laws. The authorities sit there like spiders, lurking in the fine mesh of ordinances, and it's only a matter of time before we fall prey to them. Nor are they satisfied if we've lost a leg already. We must lose our whole lives. The government, as we now see, is no longer something high above us and remote from our lives. Rather, it has all the earthly weaknesses, and no line to God. Above all, we have seen that it's not a consistent force. It encompasses the Courts and the Police and who knows how many other ministries besides. The War Minister may give someone a medal, but the Police will still lock him up. The Court may summons him, but that doesn't prevent a Police Inspector from doing the same thing. And so a fair few of us have become heathens and godless anarchists.

Sometimes Andreas thought he ought to ask for another hearing. And once, when the Prison Governor came on his weekly tour of inspection, Andreas told him his story. The Prison Governor was a very stern man, but he believed the existence of the state depended on the measure of justice it allowed within its borders. He had a statement taken from Andreas, and promised to 'get things moving.'

From that day forth, Andreas Pum had a new, faint measure of hope in his breast. He didn't know where he would go now. He had indeed lost the most important thing that a free man needs to begin a new life in good heart: faith, the home of the spirit. His body had no home either. He had to divorce Katharina. She had probably already filed the papers herself. Should he go back to Willi? Become a street beggar? Would he have his permit returned? Or wouldn't it be better if he just stayed in his cell, voluntarily, for the rest of his life?

One day, he woke very early. He didn't know the time, but it was before six o'clock, because that was when the prisoners were woken up. He felt the pain in his leg. There must be some change in the weather on the way. Suddenly he heard quiet plinking drops. It was raining.

Andreas stood up. He buckled on his crutch and stood

under the window. Now he could clearly hear the rain. If the window embrasure hadn't been so deep, it would even have been drumming on the glass. As it was, though, there was just the odd drop striking one of the bars. But that much he did know: it was raining.

Suddenly a day from Andreas's youth loomed up out of the wreckage of the years. He had got up in the middle of the night, full of disquiet and expectation, and had found that the grip of the long winter was broken. Just as he could hardly wait for morning then, so he couldn't now either. What was the cause of his commotion? For years and years he had lived through the regular changes of the seasons, and for more than thirty years now, the first spring rains had made little impression on him. For that, he had to go far back into his forgotten childhood.

And he saw the narrow lane of the very small town where he was born, and how it welcomed the arriving spring, sending small children playing to greet it, and putting out great barrels to catch the rainwater; how it opened its blocked gutters, and how the rain poured into them and disappeared underground in wild, rapturous, bubbling, gurgling floods, how it demolished the last dirty crusts of snow on the edges of the pavement, dissolving them, sweeping them away.

Ah, spring was coming, and he couldn't witness it. The world was changing, and he was in prison.

Just then the guard knocked, and Andreas called out 'Here!' so promptly that the cautious official unlocked his door and looked at Andreas already dressed, with surprise and suspicion. 'Up already?' asked the guard.

'My knee was hurting me!' replied Andreas.

'Exercise is canceled today!' said the guard, and locked the door again.

Oh, why was there no exercise today?

Slowly the darkness lightened to the familiar charcoal gray. Day dawned. The rain grew quieter. All at once a bird began twittering. A whole flock of birds twittered. A gang of sparrows pressed up against the bars. They screeched at each other, and beat their wings.

Andreas watched them and smiled. He smiled like a proud grandfather, watching his grandchildren playing. Sparrows had never meant anything to him before. Now it seemed he had to pay off an old debt to them. How he would have liked to feed them a few crumbs.

He decided to ask the guard.

When his breakfast was brought, he asked the guard to stay a moment.

'Listen,' he said, 'will you bring me a ladder? I want to put out some bread crumbs for the birds.'

If Andreas had asked him for the keys to all the cells, his astonishment would hardly have been any greater. He had been a prison guard here for twenty-six years. Of all the thousands of prisoners in his charge, not one had ever given voice to such an outrageous request. Suspicious as his profession had made him to be, the prison guard at first suspected a ruse on the part of the prisoner. He shone his torch on Andreas to study his expression.

'What made you think of that?' he asked.

'I feel so sorry for the little birdies!' said Andreas, with such a tremulous voice that the guard began to think he had truly lost his mind.

'Don't be ridiculous!' he said. 'God will look after the birds. You'd do better to eat your ration yourself!'

'Do you think?' said Andreas. 'Are you so certain that God will look after them?'

'They're not your responsibility!' replied the guard. 'Nor mine either. What are the laws for? I know my job. I'm not allowed to go bringing ladders into cells. If you're sick in the head, you need to report to the prison doctor! I'll put you down on the list, and he'll come and take a look at you. If the prison governor will allow it, he might let you feed the birds. But for that, you need to write him a petition.'

'I'd like to write him a petition then!' said Andreas.

The guard noted his wish in his duty book. An hour later, he came back with ink, paper, and a desk. 'Now write your petition,' he said, 'the governor has given you leave.'

Andreas asked the guard for help. The guard lit a candle and put on his spectacles. Then he dictated:

To the Esteemed Prison Directorate,
The undersigned herewith applies for permission to put out bread and sundry leftovers on the sill of his window once a day for the birds, and particularly the sparrows.
Signed: Andreas Pum,
Presently Serving Sentence

The guard pocketed the piece of paper.

In the afternoon, the prison doctor came by. He wondered about the mental condition of Andreas Pum. He began a conversation with the prisoner. Andreas took the opportunity to acquaint the doctor with his story, too.

The doctor was comforting. The Director, he said, would certainly get things moving. Andreas could have every confidence in him.

'But you won't be allowed to feed the sparrows! That kind of thing is too much trouble. You can't expect them to carry a ladder into your cell every day!'

'Then what did I write my petition for?'

'Those are the rules. If you have a request, you have to put it in writing. But that doesn't mean to say it's going to be granted.' The doctor smiled. He was a stout, elderly gentleman with gray stubble on his cheeks and a double chin. He wore old-fashioned gold-rimmed spectacles.

'You should leave the sparrows in God's hands!'

'Oh, doctor,' Andreas said sadly. 'Some people say: Let's leave this man in God's hands! And then God doesn't do anything to help him!'

The doctor smiled again. 'Philosophizing doesn't do you any good. You don't have the strength for it. You should have faith, my friend!' The doctor understood that he was dealing with a fool; but he knew he was a harmless fool. Anyway, there were only another three weeks of his sentence to go. So he decided to leave Andreas to himself and his philosophical thoughts. Besides, the doctor was expecting his niece tonight. He was meeting her at the station, and he had to go home before that. And, being of a philanthropical bent, he shook hands with Andreas.

Later that day, perhaps shortly before nightfall, Andreas saw the sky lighten. There was even a scrap of bright blue he could see through the dirty little window. And the sparrows were racketing again.

Then he heard the light trot of a small carriage that he heard every day at this time.

Although it was only February, he thought the buds on the willows and chestnuts would already be quite big. He thought of them with as much tenderness as he had thought of the birds. He promised himself he would go for a long walk as soon as he was set free.

That night, he had trouble getting to sleep. His knee hurt

him. The wind was howling outside and in the long prison corridors.

The next day was inspection again. The Director told him that things were looking promising. There might be a decision in two weeks. Then Andreas would get out a week early. A new case was being opened. Andreas could take his grievance to Court. Then they would see he had been treated unfairly, and his name would be cleared. He, the Director, was going to write him a glowing reference anyway. One such as he had never yet written for anybody. As far as feeding the sparrows went, that sort of thing didn't happen here. After all, it was a prison, not a bird sanctuary.

Just then the Director discovered that the bucket into which Andreas performed his bodily functions was not by the window, where it ought to be, but next to the bench, and because the Director loved Order almost as much as he loved Humanity, he said sternly: 'But that's no reason to neglect your duties!' And, just like Willi, he added: 'The rules are the rules!'

He walked out, and behind him the guard's saber rattled.

Chapter 16

EACH DAY WAS MORE beautiful than the last.

You noticed it not only in the yard, during daily exercise. You even noticed it slightly less in the yard. The air there was stale, and even though the sky arced above its high walls, it was as though there was an invisible ceiling over it. The sun never penetrated it. Hence its bricks were always slightly damp, as though they were sweating. It was a sickness of the bricks.

Every day the sparrows came by the cell window in great flocks, as though to remind Andreas of his promise. It pained him that they did. He looked up and sorrowfully surveyed the noisy little creatures. He spoke to them in silence, and his heart communed with them while his lips didn't move. My dear little birds, for decades you were nothing to me, and I was as indifferent to you as I was to the yellow horse dung in the middle of the streets that was your sustenance. I heard your twittering, of course, but it might have been the buzzing of bees for all I cared. I didn't know you could feel hunger. I barely knew that people, my own species, could feel hunger. I barely knew what pain was, even though I fought in the War, and lost one leg at the knee. Perhaps I wasn't truly human. Or perhaps my heart was sleeping, and I was sick. That happens. The heart is asleep, it ticks and tocks, but in all other respects it might as well be dead. My poor brain had no thoughts of its own. Nature hasn't blessed me with sharp wits, and my feeble intellect was betrayed by my parents, my school, my teachers, the Sergeant Major and the Captain, and the newspapers I was given to read. Don't be cross with me, little birds! I obeyed the laws of my country because I supposed wiser heads than mine had thought of them, and a great justice administered them in the name of our Lord and Creator. Oh – I had to live for more than forty years to see that in the light of freedom I was blind, only now, in the darkness of my prison cell, have I learned to see. I wanted to feed you, but I wasn't allowed to. Why not? Because no prisoner before me had ever expressed such a wish. Oh, maybe they were younger than me, and quicker and more agile, and when they saw you they didn't think of your hunger, my birds, but of their own freedom, and I know now why you are so dear to me. And I know why I was unaware of you when I still had my liberty. It was because, even though I was one-legged and old and stupid, I resembled you and I had no idea that there were a thousand prisons waiting for me, lurking in different parts of the country. You see! I want to share my bread with you, but the rules forbid that. That's what people say when they mean prison. Do you know what rules are, little birds?

Night attached itself to day, and then melted in the grayly victorious morning. Andreas stopped counting days. Years divided him from his approaching freedom. And while he longed for it to come, it did him good to believe it never would. He immersed himself in his pain and wept for himself as for a dead friend. He loved his torments like loyal enemies. He hated his bygone years like treacherous friends.

One day he was released.

Although he modestly and humbly thanked the director of the institution, and shook his hand when he offered it, he did still, hours later, feel the pressure of the mighty director's hand like a hostile power, and the will of the State and the authorities not to let go of its victim. Andreas conceived a deep distrust of the law and its representatives, and he already began to fear the new hearing. Had he not suffered injustice the first time? Would he not be locked away again? He felt like fleeing. The whole endless scope of the world was suddenly revealed to him; he saw America, Australia, and the strange places of the world; and his regained freedom felt like prison; he saw the land he lived in and where he had been hurt as a prison yard in which he was temporarily allowed to walk around, before being put back in his cell.

He made his way to the suburban station, and, with childish defiance, he bought himself a second-class ticket. For the first time he sat at ease on green cushions, reclining in a wide corner seat, with his elbow on soft, swelling leather, and he was glad that he was sitting there, which was not his place, that he was perpetrating an injustice, and that he was claiming something that was not his. He was rebelling against the unwritten and still sacred laws of earth and railway, and his truculent expression betrayed the fact to his silent and well-dressed fellow passengers. They moved aside for him, and Andreas rejoiced. He got up, he thought he ought to inspect and avail himself of all the amenities of second-class travel, so he got up to look for the toilet in the passage. It was locked. He called the conductor, who was dozing peacefully in his own compartment and, quite the outraged gentleman, ordered him to open it up. The conductor even managed a word of apology.

Andreas stepped in, and straightway recoiled. There,

looking back at him from the narrow mirror facing the door, was an old man with a white beard and a yellow, wrinkled face. The old man reminded him of evil magicians in fairy tales, who command fear and respect, and whose white patri- archal beard is the emblem of a treacherous love, a feigned goodness, and a deceitful honesty. Andreas thought he could remember the color of his eyes: had they not once been blue? Now they sparkled with green malignity. Does prison air affect even the color of one's eyes?

But why should his eyes remain unaltered, if his brown hair had turned white in a matter of weeks in prison? A matter of weeks? Didn't his imposing whiteness prove that he had spent long years there?

So he was an old man now, incapable of beginning a new life, close to death. Well, let it come. He would go back to prison of his own accord and die there. He had only a very little life left.

He went back to his seat. The other passengers made room for him again. They must have been talking about him; their silence was so abrupt and uncomfortable. Andreas looked out the window like someone traveling to his death, taking leave of the colorful pageant of this world. He was sad, a little. Even the ugly plank fences and advertisement billboards he viewed with the pain of eternal separation.

And even so, a new hope woke in his soul as he walked out of the station. He saw the joyful bustle of the great metropo- lis. He saw, over the tangle of carts and horses and people, the new sun of the approaching spring. And even though he was a white-haired cripple, he didn't give up his defiance. Facing death, he clung to life in order to rebel: against the world, against the authorities, against the Government, against God.

Chapter 17

WILLI WASN'T ASLEEP, even though it was midday, which was the time of his best and deepest sleep. Andreas didn't need to knock. Willi had heard the thump of the crutch out in the corridor. He opened the door and gave a start when he saw the white hair.

But with the gruff blitheness that was typical of him, and that greeted Andreas like a friendly shove in the chest, Willi came up with some noisy and good-humored pleasantry. He plied Andreas with sausage and jokes. He fetched a large pair of scissors, tied a towel round Andreas's neck, and with barber-like antics, started trimming his white beard into a patriarchal shovel. Andreas saw himself in the mirror, and was quite in awe of himself. 'You look like the director of an orphanage!' said Willi.

Thereupon, Willi began to dress. Andreas watched in astonishment as a light check suit was produced from the recesses of a wardrobe; a light brown stiff hat with a broad, ribbed silk ribbon, and a silk sun-yellow tie. Before long, Willi stood before him like a picture from a fashion magazine. His rather overlarge hands were in brown leather gloves, whose stitching creaked softly. Under his arm he held a bendy, yellow, gold-headed cane. Finally Willi said: 'Good-bye! I'm just going on my rounds! You have a sleep! Don't worry about anything!'

He tipped his hat and locked the door behind him. Then he went 'on his rounds.'

The past five weeks had seen a dramatic change in Willi's life. Even if by nature we are given to idleness, it sometimes happens that we are suddenly taken by the desire to work and to earn money. Whether the spring has aroused this new desire in us, or our own nature tires of inactivity and demands a change, quite irrespective of the seasons – one day a chance occurrence will drive us out of our apathy, we go out onto the street, we return to the world and enter the arena, with keen, fresh, and rested faculties.

A change had shaken Willi up. He had always had an enterprising nature. He knew what gifts he had. He had often thought of exploiting the temper of the times. He saw young people of average intelligence and a desire to get rich start up some business or other, a trade in safety matches or toilet soap, for instance, and quickly make their fortunes. He didn't need to hide from the police for the rest of his life, on account of his old peccadilloes. He knew how to fake passports, and he looked very different now than he did four years ago, when he'd staged that break-in in the Basteistrasse. His photograph wasn't displayed on any of the advertising columns in the city anymore. He had nothing to fear, really.

These thoughts came to him one night when Klara came home and told him the old man in the gents' toilet at the Café Excelsior had died. Klara shyly suggested to him that he might, just for a few weeks, take over the job as lavatory attendant. Willi declined. Spring was on the way. The racing season was starting. There was plenty of money to be made. In spring a man of his gifts did not undertake to mind a shithouse for want of something better to do.

Willi went off for three days. First, he raised some

investment capital from a store where a half-deaf widow sold coffee beans and malt. That was no trouble. He walked in, leaned over the counter, made sheep's eyes at her, and served a few customers without being asked to. Then he helped her lock up the shop, turned the lights out, and with his left hand fiddled around with her skirts, while he helped himself from the till with his right. Then he made for the great cafés of the city, talked to the managers and proprietors, and wherever he went, found shortcomings and abuses: either the toilets were badly looked after, or they weren't looked after at all. He was quite appalled at the resulting danger to public health, and promised to see what he could do. The following morning he assembled a band of idlers and war invalids off the streets, and with expert eye and pitiless judgment, set about selecting the most reliable of their number. Not finding much suitable material that way, he didn't shun the long walk out to the old people's home. That was where the most respectable old boys and girls lived. He wrote out some slips of paper, gave them each a little down payment, ran to the drugstores, ordered soaps, nail files, tooth powder, sponges and hair brushes for the big cafés, and once outside, realized that, almost by accident, he had picked up a few bottles of eau de cologne as well. He quickly brought them home to safety and erected a pyramid of them on the shelf over his bed. Then he announced to the various café managements that he had taken over the 'organization of all cloakrooms, ladies' and gentlemen's toilets.' And three days later, he collected his first income. He now had his people in every café. If the toilets were already 'occupied,' he set up cloakrooms. He called on officials in his light check suit, waved his cane around, invited constables to a glass of beer, followed by a shot of schnapps, and was given a license in the fine-sounding name. Wilhelm Klinckowstrom, which actually belonged to a dead soldier whose military papers Willi had managed to secure. Henceforth, he was known as Herr Klinckowstrom, and sometimes he even added a quiet 'von' to that already distinguished-sounding name. He rented an 'elegantly furnished room' in a desirable part of town, bought a typewriter, and installed Klara as his 'secretary.' Every day she made her way from her old place to the new one, and slowly she learned to type. Willi dictated unimportant letters to her at the top of his voice, and from time to time he would shout at her. He paid the landlady punctually, but insisted on impeccable cleanliness, under his watchword: 'The rules are the rules.' Klara gave up her other job and her nocturnal profession as well. Willi turned out to be a faithful and painstaking swain. They were getting married in May. Willi bought dresses, summer hats, goldbug shoes and silk stockings, pajamas and brassieres, all in the sheerest fabrics. In every one of 'his' places, Willi was a popular and well-treated guest. He was very useful. He was able to deal with the police; he hired musicians and bandleaders at competitive rates. Having thought he might one day emigrate to South America, he started telling everyone he'd lived in Brazil for fifteen years. He gave minutely detailed accounts of life in Brazil, and painted such a wonderful picture of the country that he felt a powerful longing to go there. He told Klara of his plan. For some weeks she'd been very happy, and so she agreed to everything. She even remembered she had an old aunt, and visited her with Willi, introducing him as her intended, Herr Klinckowstrom. The aunt was given a small allowance. Business was booming. Willi bought some cloth and silk dolls for the ladies' toilets. They went well. People saw how all the ladies, whether young or not, returned from a trip to the toilet clutching a little doll. There was plenty to do. From time to time, one of the oldsters, plucked out of his senile torpor and unable to stand the rackety nightlife, would kick off. A replacement had to be found. Some were dishonest. Willi would hand them over to the police, without any messing about. The rules were the rules.

So miraculously had fate changed Willi's life. He became a wealthy man. He only rarely stole now, and then only to test his adroitness. Generally, without stopping to think about it much, he 'bought the best.' He adored tropical fruit. He smoked Brazilian cigars. From old habit, he still carried his knuckle-duster, which had seen him through quite a few adventures. He was impeccably clean-shaven, and, in time, found favor in soft, dark, well-cut suits of unobtrusive distinction. The most expensive tailors made them for him. Sometimes Willi wore a monocle, and, when he had some writing to do, a pair of horn-rimmed spectacles, which gave his features an expression of blatant intelligence. Because he liked his spectacles, he would often sit in cafés, writing needless letters and accounts. Finally, he had the idea of writing articles for the newspapers. He wrote a series of 'Experiences in the underworld,' which bore the mark of authenticity and firsthand knowledge, and whose stylistic imperfections were quietly ironed out by the subs. Willi paid calls on the editors. As an old Brazil hand and general man of the world, he wasn't expected to write flawlessly. That was perfectly understandable.

Willi decided to engage Andreas at the Café Halali. This establishment was just in the process of jettisoning its original identity and setting itself up on a new footing. It had previously been a watering hole for old huntsmen and lovers of the chase. Now Willi was introducing a band. The old huntsmen gradually wandered off to the eternal hunting grounds. A new clientele of young folks and prettily made-up girls began to take their place. The owner had a wall taken down, thereby converting two quiet rooms into a single noisy one. Willi had the idea of setting up an elevated platform for the musicians. That required planning permission from the zoning authorities. Zoning authorities? No problem for Willi. He got permission to put up an entire balcony. He obtained a cheap loan, and was paid a commission by both parties. For the cloakroom he secured the services of an elderly lady from a convenience in the public sector, who had already been there for five years, and had just reached the age at which the female soul celebrates a kind of second spring, and was crying out for a change. All that was needed now was an old man for the gents'. In Willi's opinion, Andreas Pum was an outstanding candidate for the post.

That evening, Willi showed Andreas around his new apartment. He made the old man swear never to betray anything of the past. From that day forth, he was to address Willi as Herr von Klinckowstrom. Andreas was amazed by these profound changes. Stunned by the new magnificence, he almost thought Willi really was some Herr von Klinckowstrom. And so he began to call him by that name, which bestowed a little of its glory on those who said it. He addressed Klara as Lady Klinckowstrom. Willi turned the talk to business. 'Where's your new uniform?' he asked. 'At home – at her place,' said Andreas. 'Go and get it!' ordered Willi. But Andreas was scared. So Willi drove straight over to Frau Katharina's in his automobile.

The door was opened by Deputy Inspector Vinzenz Topp. From that, Willi concluded that Andreas had that young man to thank for his misfortune. He introduced himself as Herr von Klinckowstrom, and was glad to notice a quick shudder of awe go through the sinewy form of the underconstable, and that his chest began to swell. Thereupon he demanded Andreas's clothes and 'the rest of his property.' It transpired that Katharina had sold the hurdy-gurdy some time ago. The new uniform was still around. Willi threatened to go to court over the hurdy-gurdy, and thereby secured the immediate surrender of the uniform. He whistled, and the chauffeur, with whom he had decided upon that as a signal, approached. Willi handed him the suit, said a menacing 'Good evening,' and left. The Deputy Inspector had no doubt that he had just been visited by a great man.

The uniform on its own wasn't enough. Andreas explained that he no longer had his cross. Willi averred that he couldn't work in a toilet without it. He was aware of the secret connection between lavatory and patriotic feeling, and had a keen sense of the value of having a decorated individual in a john. The following morning, he scooped up five medals in a junk shop, among them a gold and silver star on purple, red-and-white-striped, and crimson ribbons. Andreas had to sew them on his jacket.

Two days later, he entered his service in the Café Halali toilets.

Chapter 18

ANDREAS PUM SAT surrounded by blue tiled walls and full-length mirrors, next to a blue scale. From the taps over the three china washbasins there was a steady drip of water, the plinking sound breaking the white, antiseptic silence, and it was like drops of time falling into a pool of eternity. On a little table was a pile of hand towels, ironed flat and neatly stacked, and bars of soap were formed up into an artistic, lofty, and still solid pyramid. In a glass wall cabinet were bottles of scent, games of dice, spinning tops made of brass and steel, a traveling domino set, and little sets of cards for tricks. For all of that, Willi received a commission. Andreas sold it for him. To liven up the toilet a little, the café owner had acquired a parrot. He was called Ignatz, and he had a green back with a violet shimmer, a reddish cap, and a white neck ruff. The parrot said 'Good morning' or 'Good evening' when a client entered the toilet. In slow times, especially the afternoon when there were no clients, Andreas would converse with the intelligent bird. They had plenty to talk about, Andreas and Ignatz. The parrot sat in a cage with the door left open, but he didn't care to make any excursions farther than the wall cabinet, which had a triangular gable at the top.

The parrot liked to sit up there and rub his beak thoughtfully with a claw.

Andreas remembered the time he had wanted to have such a bird along with his hurdy-gurdy. The conclusion he drew was that oftentimes a man's desires are fulfilled too late, by which time he's got old and indifferent. The parrot was very musical. When the band struck up in the café, Ignatz began to whistle. There were some tunes he especially liked, and others that roused him. If one was played that he didn't care for, his feathers bristled, his red velvet cap fluffed up, and he started flapping his wings so wildly that his colored feathers flew, and the soap pyramid started to tremble. That would happen to an extraordinary degree with the National Anthem, and with some other martial tunes. It appeared that Ignatz was a pacifist, and criminally unpatriotic to boot. Andreas was secretly delighted. He no longer cared for patriotic music either, and he thought bitterly and sarcastically of the time when he, with his hurdy-gurdy, had even tried to disseminate it further.

Ah yes, Ignatz, we're rebels, the pair of us. Unfortunately it won't do either of us any good. I'm an old cripple, and you're a helpless bird, and we'll never change the world. If I was to tell you how much I've suffered in my life, what I experienced during the War and in prison, how my eyes were opened when I was in my cell, and how I finally decided to become an active and vigorous heathen, only to see in the mirror in the suburban train that I'd become too old for all that! All my friends are still alive, and young and healthy. But I'm condemned to die, and when you beat your wings as wildly as you do, I fancy it's Death I'm hearing at my back.

The parrot looked dreamily and wistfully and completely calmly at Andreas. Then, as though to cheer up the old man, he began to whistle. His whistling was perfectly idiosyncratic, following its own compositional laws, as though muddling up the different notes on the scale, and he warbled the high notes in a rapid and repetitious trill. Then, with a quiet scream, he jumped onto Andreas's shoulder, and begged for a sugar lump, which Andreas broke up into tiny fragments for him.

Andreas was on the skids. He looked like a man of seventy. His snowy beard hung down as far as the colorful ribbons on his chest, which gave him the look of an ancient warrior. White moss sprouted from his ears. He had a loud, hacking cough, and after each fit of coughing he almost passed out, as exhausted as a child with a fever. He had to sit down for a few minutes, while the mirrors and the lights and the gleaming tiles slowed down and finally came to a stop in their accustomed places. These strange orbitings reminded Andreas of the last turns of a carousel, a memory that surfaced from his childhood. It was compounded, too, by the music from the café, for the most part muffled like a heavenly choir, which resounded at full volume each time a client came in through the door. Andreas often fell asleep. He dreamed vividly and often, and the images from his dreams were etched in his mind when he awoke. Soon he wasn't really able to distinguish between waking and dream, and he took his dreams to be reality, and reality for a dream. He didn't even see the faces of the clients anymore; he brushed their clothes, handed them soap and towels and brushes, and didn't hear what they said to him, didn't thank them for tips, and didn't count his takings. He didn't sell much of Willi's merchandise either, he didn't have any 'patter,' he didn't 'charm' the customer, as Willi asked him to when he came 'on his rounds.' It was only by grace of their old friendship that he was allowed to keep his job.

The small toilet window opened out onto a courtyard that had a chestnut tree standing in the middle of it, reminding Andreas of other courtyards where he had once played. Now the buds were growing, they were swelling visibly, becoming fat and full, and the birds hung in the branches, mating and bickering. Andreas scattered crumbs for them and gazed out at the spring, which, half hidden, pathetic but still rich, unfurled in all the splendor that the paved courtyard would allow since the sunbeams only penetrated it in the afternoons. When a client came in, Andreas had to shut the window, for decency's sake, as the kitchen windows were directly opposite, and the female kitchen staff had the habit of seeming to peer out inquisitively.

His knee hurt, the padding on the leg should have been replaced long ago. His back hurt him too, for less obvious reasons; the damp brought on his old rheumatic pains, knots of gout formed in his fingers, and his chest felt under such pressure that his heart seemed to stop for seconds at a time, till Andreas sometimes thought he was already dead. Then he would awake with a start, to find himself still alive, but with the sensation of no longer being on the earth. It took a fresh pain to remind him he was still among the living. He remembered that the dead, because they have no body, know no pain, and are pure spirit. He spent long and lonely hours pondering these questions, seeking an explanation for the manifest unfairness and mistakes of God, considering the possibilities of rebirth, and beginning to formulate various requests, as though he were already facing the Almighty, and the choice of his next incarnation. He decided he would like to be a revolutionary, someone who makes fiery speeches and sweeps across the country with fire and sword, to avenge injustice. He read about such matters in the newspapers that the café supplied him with. They were generally a couple of days old by that stage, and the news he got was no longer news when he chopped the newspapers into rectangles and hung them on nails in tidy packages. Willi was constantly reminding him to economize on expensive toilet tissue.

He got home late at night. He was now living in Willi's old room by himself, but he didn't like being at home without company. So he asked for permission to take the café parrot home with him at night. He carried the bird in its cage, draping a warm blanket over it when it was raining and the nights were cold. The parrot slept all the way, and only woke up in the room, when it sensed the light coming in through its heavy covers. Then it murmured a word or two, as a man might do in sleep or half sleep, and Andreas soothed it by speaking to it gently and kindly.

Once Andreas saw some burglars in the night, but he didn't tell the policeman he saw standing on the street corner. The burglars were working on the door of a shop. Andreas felt quietly pleased. It seemed to him that burglars have the secret purpose of forcibly redressing the injustices of the world. When his newspapers told him about murders and thefts and robberies, he rejoiced. Criminals, the 'heathens,' had become his secret allies. They knew nothing of it. But he was their friend, their patron. Sometimes he dreamed a fugitive criminal came to him in his toilet. He would joyfully help the man to make good his escape through the window and into the yard to freedom.

By now the April days had become warm, rain-heavy, and sweet with promise. At night, Andreas breathed a distant scent carried on the wind, and his limbs felt more tired than usual. He lost interest in many things. Even the resumption of his case no longer interested him. He was old, even older than he knew himself. He was already pushing on into the next life, even while he still trod the cobbled pavements of this one. His soul dreamed its way into the hereafter, which was its place. It returned to his real existence with dismay.

His pains got worse, his cough became more of a hack; the fits of it grew longer. Each day he forgot what had happened the day before. He talked to himself. Sometimes he forgot the parrot, and was startled to hear its crackling voice. Death cast its great blue shadow over Andreas.

Then one day a Court summons arrived for him. Just like the first, it bore the imposing official seal of a white eagle spreading its pinions on a blood-red ground, and, even though the address had been scrawled, proof of the busyness and haste of the courts, the document still conveyed the dignity attached to all postage-free official missives. Andreas read it. Once again, he was invited to attend at ten in the morning.

He remembered his old sufferings, he worked on a speech, he drew up a comprehensive accusation. 'High Court,' he planned to say, 'I am a victim of conditions that are of your making. Condemn me. I confess, I am a rebel. I am old, I haven't much longer to live. But I would not have been afraid, even if I had been young.' Many thousands of beautiful and memorable phrases came to him. He sat on his stool next to the blue scale, mumbling to himself. A gentleman called for soap, and he didn't hear. Ignatz fluttered onto his shoulder and asked for sugar. Andreas didn't feel it.

Chapter 19

A CHURCH CLOCK struck ten. A second clock chimed in. With long, drawn-out, plangent strokes, a third. Many churches, all the churches of the city, threw peals of bells down onto the copper roofs.

Andreas stood before the judge. He had just handed his summons to the court usher, who carried it solemnly across to the clerk of the court on tiptoe, so as not to disturb the contemplative peace of the court by the heavy clump of his evidently hobnailed boots, but even so there was something weighty in his walk, as in the march of a silent ghost. The clerk was ancient and had a crooked shoulder. He appeared to be shortsighted as well. His nose almost touched the desk on which he was writing, and the top of his pen protruded, thin and menacing, like a sharpened spear, over the top of his head. The proceedings had not been started yet, but the quill rustled and darted over the paper, as though copying down all the depositions of the centuries.

The judge sat, flanked by two fair-skinned, well-nourished men with shiny, bald pates. Andreas wished he knew what was going on in their minds. They looked like twins, the only distinction between them being that the one had an upturned mustache, while the other's made a horizontal line. The judge himself was clean-shaven. He had an impassive face of granite majesty, like a dead emperor's. It was gray as weathered sandstone. His large gray eyes were as old as the world, and seemed to be able to gaze through walls at distant millennia. Below his smooth, angular forehead, his eyebrows were not curved as with most people, but made two long, horizontal, charcoal lines. His thin lips were pinched shut, wide and blood red. It was a face that might have looked heartless and implacable, had the middle of its powerful masculine chin not held an appealing, almost childlike dimple. He wore a black gown with a narrow, even blacker, velvet trim.

On a raised dais, between two thick white candles of unequal height, stood a cross, yellow and massive, as though hewn from great blocks. It looked to Andreas as though this cross had been built up out of the bars of soap that Willi had given him to sell. But that was just a momentary error. Andreas could see that a cross like that could never be made from soap, and that it was a sin to imagine that it might be.

He looked forward to the proceedings eagerly. From time to time the door opened. Then Andreas saw, waiting on a bench in the corridor, his wife, Katharina, little Anni, the gentleman from the tram platform, and curiously also the apple-cheeked man who had purchased the donkey. They were the witnesses. But where were the policeman and the conductor?

The judge read out the name: Andreas Pum, and mumbled some dates, his faith, place of birth, and occupation. Then he raised his voice, which was deep and soft, and he said a few words that seemed draped in velvet. Andreas had only listened to the timbre of the voice, not to what the judge had said. He knew, nevertheless, that he had been asked to make his statement.

Suddenly he remembered that he was still wearing the

fancy medals on his chest that Willi had bought him. He ripped them off, and held them clutched in his hand. At the same time, he noticed that the walls of the courtroom were covered in pale blue tiles, just like the walls in the toilets at the Café Halali. There was a breeze from the ceiling that seemed to be immeasurably high, a cool and fragrant breeze, as from a shady barbershop in summer, but he didn't dare look up.

He cleared his throat and began to speak, beginning with a description of the scene on the tram platform. But the judge put out his slender and beautiful hand, which extended white and noble from the wide sleeves of his toga, and motioned him to stop. At the same time, a voice sounded, soft and dark, even though he hadn't moved his lips. This struck Andreas as very remarkable. Once, as a boy, he had been to see a ventriloquist, but he had had rather a growly voice. And anyway, a judge certainly wasn't a ventriloquist. How, though, was it possible that with lips closed, he still clearly and distinctly pronounced the words:

'Andreas, what is burdening you?'

The informal '*du*' with which he'd been addressed was the next thing to surprise Andreas. But then he remembered he was a little boy. He was in short trousers. He had both his legs, and he was barefooted. His knees were scraped, sore and bleeding from a recent fall, playing on the riverbank.

He was just considering this strange transformation when music resounded. Initially, it reminded him of his hurdy-gurdy. But then the sounds swelled, they flowed and poured and broadened; collapsed again, began to whisper, removed themselves, and then turned back. The room was full of people. They knelt down. The candles on either side of the cross burned with golden flames and spread a fragrance of incense and stearin.

With that, Andreas understood that he had died, and was standing before the Heavenly Judge. Nor was he a boy anymore either. He was the only person standing among a thousand kneeling in the whole room. He took a step forward on his crutch, but it made no sound. Andreas saw that he was standing on soft clouds. He remembered the speech he had prepared for his earthly hearing. A powerful anger welled up in him, his complexion reddened, and his soul gave birth to words, angry purple words, a thousand, ten thousand, a million words. They were not words he had ever heard or thought or read. They had slept deep within him, tamed by his miserable intellect, atrophied under the cruel veneer of his life. Now they sprouted and fell from him like blossoms from a tree. The solemn and mournful music continued softly in the background. Andreas heard it as he listened to the roaring of his own speech:

I have awakened from my servile meekness into red, rebellious obstinacy. I would deny You, God, if I were alive and not standing before You. But seeing You with my own eyes and hearing You with my own ears, I must do worse than deny You: I must revile You! You spawn millions like me in Your senseless fertility, and they grow up, credulous and bowed, they suffer blows in Your name, they salute Emperors, Kings, and Governments in Your name, they suffer purulent wounds of bullets in their bodies, and let three-edged bayonets drill their hearts, or they sink under the yoke of Your industrious days, sour Sundays cheaply frame their brutal weeks, they are hungry and silent, their children wither, their wives grow ugly and unfaithful, the laws proliferate across their path like treacherous creepers, their feet are ensnared in the tangle of Your edicts, they fall and pray to You, and You do not raise them up. Your white hands should be red really, Your stone face contorted, Your upright body twisted, like the bodies of my comrades with bullets in their spines. Others, whom You love and feed, are allowed to punish us without even having to praise You. You allow them to dispense with prayer and sacrifice, uprightness and meekness, so that they may trick us. We sustain the burdens of their wealth and their bodies, their sins and their punishments upon ourselves, their guilt and their crimes, we murder ourselves at their wish; they desire to see cripples, and we go and lose our legs at the joint; they want us sightless, so we have ourselves blinded; they want not to be heard, so we are deafened; they alone want to smell and taste, and we hurl grenades at our mouths and noses; they alone want to eat, and we mill the grain. Meanwhile You exist and are impassive? I rebel against You, not against them. It's You who are guilty, not Your accomplices. You are the master of millions of worlds, and yet don't know what to do. How impotent You are in Your omnipotence! You have billions of accounts, and make mistakes in individual items? What kind of God are You! Is Your cruelty a wisdom that it is beyond us to comprehend – then how flawed You made us! If we must suffer, why do all not suffer equally? If Your blessing is not sufficient for everyone, at least distribute it equally! I'm a sinner – but I wanted to do good! Why did You not let me feed the little birds? If You feed them Yourself, You feed them badly. Ah, I wish I could still deny You. But You exist. Single, omnipotent, implacable, the highest tribunal, eternal – and there's no hope of Your being punished, of God blowing You to a cloud, of Your heart being awoken. I don't want Your mercy! I want to go to Hell.

The last few sentences Andreas had sung in a strange, unfamiliar, and wonderful melody. The music was still playing like an orchestra of sighs.

Then the judge raised his hand, and his voice resounded: 'Do you want to be a guard in a museum, or an attendant in a municipal park, or have a concession to sell tobacco on the street corner?'

'I want to go to Hell!' repeated Andreas.

Then all at once, Mooli, the little donkey, appeared next to Andreas, pulling the hurdy-gurdy, which was playing even without anyone to crank its handle. Ignatz the parrot perched on Andreas's shoulder. The judge stood up, he loomed bigger and bigger, his gray countenance began to shine white, his red lips parted in a smile. Andreas began to cry. He didn't know if he was in Heaven or Hell.

The gentlemen's toilet of the Café Halali was locked up for the evening, and the gentlemen were told to use the ladies'. After all the customers had left for the night, Andreas Pum's body was taken away. After a few days, as there happened to be a shortage of cadavers, in spite of its missing a leg, it was taken to the Anatomical Institute, where by some mysterious chance it was given the same No. 73 that Andreas had had as a prisoner. Before the body was taken to the dissecting room, Willi came to say good-bye. He was on the point of tears when he remembered the tune he always liked to whistle.

And with the tune on his lips, he went off to find an old man for the toilet.

ABOUT THE TRANSLATOR

MICHAEL HOFMANN was born in Freiburg, Germany, and educated in England. He has translated more than eighty books from German into English since 1984, and collected many awards. Recent translations include Alfred Döblin's *Berlin Alexanderplatz* and Hans Fallada's *Little Man, What Now?* He has translated much of Joseph Roth's oeuvre and, amongst others, works by Franz Kafka, Heinrich von Kleist, Elias Canetti, Ernst Jünger, Wolfgang Koeppen, Gert Hofmann, Wim Wenders and Günter Eich. Michael Hofmann is also a poet, critic and essayist.

TITLES IN EVERYMAN'S LIBRARY

CHINUA ACHEBE
The African Trilogy
Things Fall Apart

AESCHYLUS
The Oresteia

ISABEL ALLENDE
The House of the Spirits

MARTIN AMIS
London Fields

THE ARABIAN NIGHTS

ISAAC ASIMOV
Foundation
Foundation and Empire
Second Foundation
(in 1 vol.)

MARGARET ATWOOD
The Handmaid's Tale

JOHN JAMES AUDUBON
The Audubon Reader

AUGUSTINE
The Confessions

JANE AUSTEN
Emma
Mansfield Park
Northanger Abbey
Persuasion
Pride and Prejudice
Sanditon and Other Stories
Sense and Sensibility

THE BABUR NAMA

JAMES BALDWIN
Giovanni's Room
Go Tell It on the Mountain

HONORÉ DE BALZAC
Cousin Bette
Eugénie Grandet
Old Goriot

MIKLOS BANFFY
The Transylvanian Trilogy
(in 2 vols)

JOHN BANVILLE
The Book of Evidence
The Sea (in 1 vol.)

JULIAN BARNES
Flaubert's Parrot
A History of the World in
10½ Chapters (in 1 vol.)

GIORGIO BASSANI
The Garden of the Finzi-Continis

SIMONE DE BEAUVOIR
The Second Sex

SAMUEL BECKETT
Molloy, Malone Dies,
The Unnamable

SAUL BELLOW
The Adventures of Augie March

HECTOR BERLIOZ
The Memoirs of Hector Berlioz

THE BIBLE
(King James Version)
The Old Testament
The New Testament

WILLIAM BLAKE
Poems and Prophecies

GIOVANNI BOCCACCIO
Decameron

JORGE LUIS BORGES
Ficciones

JAMES BOSWELL
The Life of Samuel Johnson
The Journal of a Tour to
the Hebrides

ELIZABETH BOWEN
Collected Stories

RAY BRADBURY
The Stories of Ray Bradbury

JEAN ANTHELME
BRILLAT-SAVARIN
The Physiology of Taste

ANNE BRONTË
Agnes Grey and The Tenant of
Wildfell Hall

CHARLOTTE BRONTË
Jane Eyre
Villette
Shirley and The Professor

EMILY BRONTË
Wuthering Heights

MIKHAIL BULGAKOV
The Master and Margarita

EDMUND BURKE
Reflections on the Revolution in
France and Other Writings

SAMUEL BUTLER
The Way of all Flesh

A. S. BYATT
Possession

JAMES M. CAIN
The Postman Always Rings Twice
Double Indemnity
Mildred Pierce
Selected Stories
(in 1 vol. US only)

ITALO CALVINO
If on a winter's night a traveler

ALBERT CAMUS
The Outsider (UK)
The Stranger (US)
The Plague, The Fall,
Exile and the Kingdom,
and Selected Essays (in 1 vol.)

PETER CAREY
Oscar and Lucinda
True History of the Kelly Gang
(in 1 vol.)

ANGELA CARTER
The Bloody Chamber
Wise Children
Fireworks
(in 1 vol.)

GIACOMO CASANOVA
History of My Life

WILLA CATHER
Death Comes for the
Archbishop (US only)
My Ántonia
O Pioneers!

BENVENUTO CELLINI
The Autobiography of
Benvenuto Cellini

MIGUEL DE CERVANTES
Don Quixote

RAYMOND CHANDLER
The novels (in 2 vols)
Collected Stories

GEOFFREY CHAUCER
Canterbury Tales

ANTON CHEKHOV
The Complete Short Novels
My Life and Other Stories
The Steppe and Other Stories

G. K. CHESTERTON
The Everyman Chesterton

KATE CHOPIN
The Awakening

CARL VON CLAUSEWITZ
On War

S. T. COLERIDGE
Poems

WILKIE COLLINS
The Moonstone
The Woman in White

CONFUCIUS
The Analects

JOSEPH CONRAD
Heart of Darkness
Lord Jim
Nostromo
The Secret Agent
Typhoon and Other Stories
Under Western Eyes
Victory

JULIO CORTÁZAR
Hopscotch
Blow-Up and Other Stories
We Love Glenda So Much and
Other Tales
(in 1 vol.)

THOMAS CRANMER
The Book of Common Prayer
(UK only)

ROALD DAHL
Collected Stories

DANTE ALIGHIERI
The Divine Comedy

CHARLES DARWIN
The Origin of Species
The Voyage of the Beagle
(in 1 vol.)

DANIEL DEFOE
Moll Flanders
Robinson Crusoe

CHARLES DICKENS
Barnaby Rudge
Bleak House
A Christmas Carol and
Other Christmas Books
David Copperfield
Dombey and Son

ANNE FRANK
The Diary of a Young Girl
(US only)

BENJAMIN FRANKLIN
The Autobiography
and Other Writings

GEORGE MACDONALD
FRASER
Flashman
Flash for Freedom!
Flashman in the Great Game
(in 1 vol.)

MAVIS GALLANT
The Collected Stories

ELIZABETH GASKELL
Mary Barton

EDWARD GIBBON
The Decline and Fall of the
Roman Empire
Vols 1 to 3: The Western Empire
Vols 4 to 6: The Eastern Empire

KAHLIL GIBRAN
The Collected Works

J. W. VON GOETHE
Selected Works

NIKOLAI GOGOL
The Collected Tales
Dead Souls

IVAN GONCHAROV
Oblomov

GÜNTER GRASS
The Tin Drum

ROBERT GRAVES
Goodbye to All That

GRAHAM GREENE
Brighton Rock
The Human Factor

DASHIELL HAMMETT
The Maltese Falcon
The Thin Man
Red Harvest
(in 1 vol.)
The Dain Curse,
The Glass Key,
and Selected Stories

THOMAS HARDY
Far From the Madding Crowd
Jude the Obscure
The Mayor of Casterbridge
The Return of the Native
Tess of the d'Urbervilles
The Woodlanders

JAROSLAV HAŠEK
The Good Soldier Švejk

NATHANIEL HAWTHORNE
The Scarlet Letter

JOSEPH HELLER
Catch-22

ERNEST HEMINGWAY
A Farewell to Arms
The Collected Stories
(UK only)

GEORGE HERBERT
The Complete English Works

HERODOTUS
The Histories

MICHAEL HERR
Dispatches (US only)

PATRICIA HIGHSMITH
The Talented Mr. Ripley
Ripley Under Ground
Ripley's Game
(in 1 vol.)

HINDU SCRIPTURES
(tr. R. C. Zaehner)

JAMES HOGG
Confessions of a Justified Sinner

HOMER
The Iliad
The Odyssey

VICTOR HUGO
The Hunchback of Notre-Dame
Les Misérables

ALEXANDER VON
HUMBOLDT
Selected Writings

ALDOUS HUXLEY
Brave New World

KAZUO ISHIGURO
The Remains of the Day

GUY DE MAUPASSANT
Selected Stories

CORMAC McCARTHY
The Border Trilogy

IAN McEWAN
Atonement

HERMAN MELVILLE
The Complete Shorter Fiction
Moby-Dick

JOHN STUART MILL
On Liberty and Utilitarianism

JOHN MILTON
The Complete English Poems

YUKIO MISHIMA
The Temple of the
Golden Pavilion

MARY WORTLEY MONTAGU
Letters

MICHEL DE MONTAIGNE
The Complete Works

THOMAS MORE
Utopia

TONI MORRISON
Beloved
Song of Solomon

LORRIE MOORE
Collected Stories

JOHN MUIR
Selected Writings

ALICE MUNRO
Carried Away: A Selection of
Stories

MURASAKI SHIKIBU
The Tale of Genji

IRIS MURDOCH
The Sea, The Sea
A Severed Head
(in 1 vol.)

VLADIMIR NABOKOV
Lolita
Pale Fire
Pnin
Speak, Memory

V. S. NAIPAUL
A Bend in the River
Collected Short Fiction (US only)
A House for Mr Biswas

R. K. NARAYAN
Swami and Friends
The Bachelor of Arts
The Dark Room
The English Teacher
(in 1 vol.)
Mr Sampath – The Printer of
Malgudi
The Financial Expert
Waiting for the Mahatma
(in 1 vol.)

IRÈNE NÉMIROVSKY
David Golder
The Ball
Snow in Autumn
The Courilof Affair
(in 1 vol.)

FLANN O'BRIEN
The Complete Novels

FRANK O'CONNOR
The Best of Frank O'Connor

BEN OKRI
The Famished Road

MICHAEL ONDAATJE
The English Patient

GEORGE ORWELL
Animal Farm
Nineteen Eighty-Four
Essays
Burmese Days, Keep the Aspidistra
Flying, Coming Up for Air
(in 1 vol.)

OVID
The Metamorphoses

THOMAS PAINE
Rights of Man
and Common Sense

ORHAN PAMUK
My Name is Red
Snow

BORIS PASTERNAK
Doctor Zhivago

SAMUEL PEPYS
The Diary of Samuel Pepys

SYLVIA PLATH
The Bell Jar (US only)

PLATO
The Republic
Symposium and Phaedrus

EDGAR ALLAN POE
The Complete Stories

MARCO POLO
The Travels of Marco Polo

HENRIK PONTOPPIDAN
Lucky Per

MARCEL PROUST
In Search of Lost Time
(in 4 vols, UK only)

PHILIP PULLMAN
His Dark Materials

ALEXANDER PUSHKIN
The Collected Stories

FRANÇOIS RABELAIS
Gargantua and Pantagruel

ERICH MARIA REMARQUE
All Quiet on the Western Front

JOSEPH ROTH
The Radetzky March

JEAN-JACQUES
ROUSSEAU
Confessions
The Social Contract and
the Discourses

SALMAN RUSHDIE
Midnight's Children

JOHN RUSKIN
Praeterita and Dilecta

PAUL SCOTT
The Raj Quartet (in 2 vols)

WALTER SCOTT
Rob Roy

WILLIAM SHAKESPEARE
Comedies Vols 1 and 2
Histories Vols 1 and 2
Romances
Sonnets and Narrative Poems
Tragedies Vols 1 and 2

MARY SHELLEY
Frankenstein

JANE SMILEY
A Thousand Acres

ADAM SMITH
The Wealth of Nations

ALEXANDER SOLZHENITSYN
One Day in the Life of
Ivan Denisovich

SOPHOCLES
The Theban Plays

MURIEL SPARK
The Prime of Miss Jean Brodie,
The Girls of Slender Means, The
Driver's Seat, The Only Problem
(in 1 vol.)

CHRISTINA STEAD
The Man Who Loved Children

JOHN STEINBECK
The Grapes of Wrath

STENDHAL
The Charterhouse of Parma
Scarlet and Black

LAURENCE STERNE
Tristram Shandy

ROBERT LOUIS STEVENSON
The Master of Ballantrae and
Weir of Hermiston
Dr Jekyll and Mr Hyde
and Other Stories

BRAM STOKER
Dracula

HARRIET BEECHER STOWE
Uncle Tom's Cabin

SUN TZU
The Art of War

ITALO SVEVO
Zeno's Conscience

GRAHAM SWIFT
Waterland

JONATHAN SWIFT
Gulliver's Travels

TACITUS
Annals and Histories

JUNICHIRŌ TANIZAKI
The Makioka Sisters

W. M. THACKERAY
Vanity Fair

HENRY DAVID THOREAU
Walden

ALEXIS DE TOCQUEVILLE
Democracy in America

LEO TOLSTOY
Collected Shorter Fiction (in 2 vols)
Anna Karenina
Childhood, Boyhood and Youth
The Cossacks
War and Peace

ANTHONY TROLLOPE
Barchester Towers
Can You Forgive Her?
Doctor Thorne
The Duke's Children
The Eustace Diamonds
Framley Parsonage
The Last Chronicle of Barset
Phineas Finn
The Small House at Allington
The Warden

IVAN TURGENEV
Fathers and Children
First Love and Other Stories
A Sportsman's Notebook

MARK TWAIN
Tom Sawyer
and Huckleberry Finn

JOHN UPDIKE
The Complete Henry Bech
Rabbit Angstrom

GIORGIO VASARI
Lives of the Painters, Sculptors and
Architects (in 2 vols)

JULES VERNE
Journey to the Centre of the Earth
Twenty Thousand Leagues under
the Sea
Round the World in Eighty Days

VIRGIL
The Aeneid

VOLTAIRE
Candide and Other Stories

HORACE WALPOLE
Selected Letters

EVELYN WAUGH
(US only)
Black Mischief, Scoop, The Loved
One, The Ordeal of Gilbert
Pinfold (in 1 vol.)
Brideshead Revisited

Decline and Fall
A Handful of Dust
The Sword of Honour Trilogy
Waugh Abroad: Collected Travel
Writing
The Complete Short Stories

H. G. WELLS
The Time Machine,
The Invisible Man,
The War of the Worlds
(in 1 vol., US only)

EDITH WHARTON
The Age of Innocence
The Custom of the Country
Ethan Frome, Summer,
Bunner Sisters
(in 1 vol.)
The House of Mirth
The Reef

PATRICK WHITE
Voss

OSCAR WILDE
Plays, Prose Writings and Poems

P. G. WODEHOUSE
The Best of Wodehouse

MARY WOLLSTONECRAFT
A Vindication of the Rights of
Woman

VIRGINIA WOOLF
To the Lighthouse
Mrs Dalloway

WILLIAM WORDSWORTH
Selected Poems (UK only)

RICHARD YATES
Revolutionary Road
The Easter Parade
Eleven Kinds of Loneliness
(in 1 vol.)

W. B. YEATS
The Poems (UK only)

ÉMILE ZOLA
Germinal

This book is set in BEMBO which was cut
by the punch-cutter Francesco Griffo
for the Venetian printer-publisher
Aldus Manutius in early 1495
and first used in a pamphlet
by a young scholar
named Pietro
Bembo.